BOOKMARKED
FOR MURDER

Marion Moore Hill

D0110017

Published 2003 by
The Fiction Works
Lake Tahoe, Nevada
www.fictionworks.com

ISBN 1-58124-031-7
Printed in the
United States of America

For Elbert,
Who helped this to happen
And who makes it matter

WHAT CRITICS ARE SAYING
about *Bookmarked for Murder*

"*Bookmarked for Murder* is beautifully written and richly detailed. Librarians make such intelligent sleuths!"
—Linda S. Bingham, *What the Librarian Heard*

"*Bookmarked for Murder* has made me a real devotee of Marion Hill mysteries. It's the kind of book I love to read: well-written; interesting, enjoyable characters; and a clear but intriguing narrative style. I'm eagerly awaiting the follow-up."
—Dr. Joseph E. Littlejohn, retired college English professor and dean

"Move over, Cassandra Mitchell, Helma Zukas, and Jordan Poteet; Juanita Wills has joined you at the checkout desk! Today's libraries are not quiet, safe havens and librarians aren't shy folk, afraid to face the dangers their inquisitiveness may bring their way. Librarian Juanita Wills takes on the local militia, racism, murder and the petty squabbles of her library staff in a mystery that mixes the coziness of small town mores with the hard-boiled edge of big city crime. But forget about a bookmark—you won't stop reading long enough to need one!"
—Jeanette Larson, Librarian, Austin (Texas) Public Library

"An enjoyable read that is difficult to put down."
—Pamala Nelson, Texas mystery fan

"Juanita Wills is reminiscent of Anne George's Southern Sisters, and the cultural tone of *Bookmarked for Murder* is Southern with an Oklahoma twist."
—Sharla Frost, Texas attorney and mystery fan

"*Bookmarked for Murder* is a very enjoyable book. The characters are well defined, and the story satisfying—well worth the read."

—Lanette Swindle, Waldenbooks store manager

"Mystery fans of Jenny Cain have something new to look forward to in Juanita Wills."

—Brenda Corbin, Oklahoma journalist

"First novels are always a treat to read and Marion Moore Hill's *Bookmarked for Murder* is no exception. Even though the setting is a small town in Oklahoma, this book could be anywhere USA . . . (its) characters have both spice and color. This is definitely a page-turner, with the reader unsure until the last exactly who the culprit is."

—Sharon Morrison, Oklahoma college reference librarian

". . . a book you will share with your friends."

—Audrey Eggers, Reviewer "Cozies, Capers & Crimes"

"A rousing good read! Marion Moore Hill captures the flavor of small town America and serves up a tantalizing dinner of murder and political intrigue, with side dishes of literary humor and gentle romance."

—Marilyn Celeste Morris, author of *Sabbath's Room*

"I read *Bookmarked for Murder* in two sittings! As a corporate librarian for almost 20 years, I especially enjoyed the fact that the main character is a librarian—and one with such pluck and wit! I'll be at the top of the list waiting to buy a copy of the sequel!" —Judy Leavitt, Iowa corporate librarian

"This novel is filled with local characters that inhabit small towns, so vivid you're positive you've met them."

—Bea Carpentieri, Florida mystery fan

Acknowledgements

Grateful thanks go to my fellow writers in three critique groups for constructive criticism, generous support and friendship: Billie and Dennis Letts, Glenda Zumwalt, the late Bob and Betty Swearengin, Brad Cushman, Chuck Ladd, Lynda Abbott, Colleen Lamb, Debbie Wilkens, Donna McMurry, Shirley Higginbotham, JoAnn Ridings, Roberta Cazzelle, Dolores White Kiser, Stan Cosby, June Proctor, Helen Dickerson, Leora Bridgewater, Renee Laney, Michael Main, Robin Murray, Deborah Mitchell, Tammy Flieger and Randy Prus; to a host of other able readers for sharing their reactions, especially Howard Starks, Kate Ball, Scottie Johnson, Toni Stiefer, Marilyn Birdsong, Alice Moore, Marilyn Crawford, Sonja Sides, Madeline Gresch, Dean Allison, Shirley Lawson, Janice Ezell, Anna Lee Locke and Diane Estep; to Charlie Stiefer, Perry Unruh and John Caldwell for valuable technical assistance; and to editor Sara Ann Freed and authors Julie Smith and Susan Wittig Albert for early suggestions and encouragement.

BOOKMARKED
FOR MURDER

Prologue

Eddie waited in a crouch, his sweaty hands clutching the M16. Clouds alternately hid and revealed a new moon, softening edges of scrub oak and barbed wire on the obstacle course. His heart galloped, his throat felt as parched as the surrounding weeds looked.

Monday night. His folks thought he was studying at Joey's house. Eddie was learning, all right, how to stay alive if he ever had to defend Oklahoma and the U.S.A.

If Gib knew how scared he was about this first live-ammo exercise, Eddie would never hear the end of it. Gib loved everything about modern warfare, from its futuristic night-vision glasses and remote-control gun emplacement to its eons-old human responses of blood, sweat and fear.

Fortunately, Gib wasn't here to observe Eddie's fright. He had gone off somewhere with the Major and a sergeant tonight.

"Ro-o-o-o-l out!" The command finally came.

Two fifty-caliber machine guns, set forty-two inches high, chattered out of the darkness ahead. Eddie worked his way forward, staying low to avoid the tracer bullets. Rocks and briars tore his hands and clothing. His rifle caught on a stabbing branch, and he paused to work it loose.

After what seemed ten miles, he arrived at the machine-gun nest, first of his squad. Tired but proud, he flung himself down against a tree, his mind wandering to his favorite daydream:

A mortar directly ahead had the unit trapped. Armed only with a knife, Eddie crawled from the ravine and around behind the enemy. As a shell thudded to the casing bottom, he stepped up and deftly slit one man's throat, then the other's. Afterwards, a properly modest Eddie was basking in his buddies' grateful praise when . . . a movement against his leg startled him. Still half in the fantasy, he froze. He was about to be attacked as he had surprised his enemies just now, and he would die.

The snake, finding a human in its path, changed course and crawled away into the brush.

Slowly, Eddie inhaled. He felt sick, struck by a sudden realization. He now knew twenty ways to kill or disable another guy, maybe one like himself, doing a job in spite of fear. What he was involved in was serious. Deadly serious.

Chapter One

Before the events of that spring, Juanita Wills would have claimed one advantage of her job was the unlikelihood of ever being a murder target. On a professionals-getting-hit-most-often list, she would have ranked librarians below cable installers and pizza delivery guys, slightly above cloistered nuns. Later she would admit, to herself only, that what happened was partly her fault, the result of what her fellow, Police Lieutenant Wayne Cleary, called her supersnoop mentality. But the main cause was someone else's hate.

One chilly evening in March Juanita strolled home from Wyndham Public Library after working late on a report. Street lights illuminated fronts of modest bungalows, while housebacks disappeared into night. Darkened windows indicated that residents were already abed. A truck rumbled by on Center Avenue one block over. A breeze carried the scent of long-dry leaves.

Ahead, Wyndham United Methodist Church stood out like a scene on a sympathy card, its white-frame facade and low spire luminous in a street lamp's glow. Juanita whistled contentedly under her breath. What could be more peaceful than a church in a small Oklahoma town on a Monday night?

"No! Don't—"

Gulping back a note, she paused mid-stride. The yell had come from the direction of the church. Now she heard scuffling noises. A crash. A muffled cry. A thud. Two soft clunks.

"What in the wide world—"

Silence, for a moment. Then running footsteps inside the building. Juanita saw the church door stood ajar, a javelin of light marking the edge.

The entry flew wide. Three men burst through. They paused just outside, lit between vestibule light and street lamp.

Juanita's breath caught in her throat. All wore dark clothing, all had their faces covered.

One started her direction, then noticing her, paused uncertainly.

"Get her!" Another strode purposefully toward Juanita.

Her heart trip-hammered. Her feet wouldn't move.

"No! Run!" The third man raced after the second, yanked on his sweater and pulled him to a stop.

The second man's fist curled mere inches from Juanita's chin. She stared into shadowy sockets in his ghostly stump of a head.

"Don't wimp out now!" he growled.

"I said run!" The third man again.

To Juanita's astonishment, her would-be attacker obeyed. He turned away, following the others around the corner of the church into an unlit brushy area. Tinder-dry foliage rustled. Twigs snapped. A voice cursed an ensnaring vine.

Quiet descended.

Juanita's heart rate slowed. She felt like a tornado survivor, dazed but vastly relieved.

She should call the police, but where from? The parsonage next door looked dark like the surrounding houses, and her own home was still four blocks away.

The church entrance yawned invitingly.

She hesitated. What had the trio been up to? Not burglary. At least they hadn't been carrying anything. Besides, this modest house of prayer must offer little to steal.

Wayne would tell her to leave and phone for help. What she considered lively curiosity, he called nosiness.

"And with your general laxness about safety, babe," he had told her once, "that could get you killed some day."

A low moan came from the direction of the sanctuary. A fourth intruder inside, wounded? Or someone else? Whoever it was sounded in pain.

She should go call for help, leave any heroics to professionals. Another groan, barely audible this time.

Then she remembered a weapon forgotten in the sudden confrontation. Since getting mugged last year in New Orleans, she had carried mace.

"*Now* I think of it." Adrenaline surging, she took the can from her shoulder bag and entered the church. Hurrying through an orderly foyer, she stopped to listen at the open sanctuary door. The sounds of distress had come from this area, but all she heard now was her own rapid breathing.

She edged into the big room. Down front in the podium area, some radiance at floor level illuminated an odd tumble of objects. That looked wrong.

Mace at the ready, she groped along the door facing for a light panel. Finding none, she tried the other side with no more success. Then she recalled hearing that when the church had been built years ago, its first pastor had had most electrical switches installed in the office to control utilities usage.

Suppressing her irritation, she crept down the sloping aisle, her nostrils registering some odor alien to the church smells of old hymnals, candle wax and furniture polish.

As she neared the front pew, her eyes swept a chaotic scene. A table lolled on one side. Headrest down across it, legs raking the air, lay a high-backed chair. Toppled candelabra snuggled between the lectern and—a man.

Wearing bathrobe and slippers, he reclined face down on a carpet runner. A large Bible sprawled open nearby, as if he had fallen asleep reading. But the dark splotch beside his ear told a different tale.

Heart drumming, Juanita knelt, set down the mace and touched his wrist. Warm. A faint pulse fluttered.

A metal flashlight four feet away, its beam fragmented by wreckage, proved to be the light source. Juanita crawled to it, pantyhosed knees scritching on the carpet, and shone it on his face.

Ferris Asher, the church's pastor. Why was he here in a dark sanctuary on a Monday night, dressed for bed and hurt?

The gash at his temple bleeding onto cheek and nose looked even worse in direct light. She must get help. As Juanita scrambled to her feet, the torch played over the wall behind the pulpit. She gasped.

A huge swastika, crudely made in paint as red as Asher's blood, appeared there. The crimson legend below said, "FAG NIGER LUVER DOER OF DEVELS WERK." The letters "G.O.L" seemed to form a signature.

Paint, that was what she had smelled. A spray can sat on the podium floor near the disfigured wall.

No time to ponder the message's meaning. Juanita laid the flashlight near the minister in case he should wake and wonder where he was, then guided by its rays hurried back up the aisle.

Outside again, she saw to her relief that a light now burned in the living room of the little stucco parsonage. She dashed up the steps and rang the bell. Almost immediately, a porch light came on. Widened eyes peered around a shade over the portal's narrow window.

The door opened, framing Mariette Asher in lamplight. She clutched together a shabby blue housecoat. Her long blonde hair, released from its usual French braid, hung loose.

"Miss Wills, isn't it? What—"

"Got to use—the phone," Juanita panted. "Your husband—"

"What about Ferris? What's happened?"

"Hurt—in the church—needs help."

Wordlessly Mariette pulled Juanita inside, pointed to a telephone and dashed out. Juanita phoned 911, then returned to the sanctuary.

Mariette knelt beside her husband, stanching blood with a patch of gauze. While getting the first-aid kit from the office, she had turned on overhead lights too. The scene now seemed less eerie, though Asher's wound looked no better.

Juanita sat beside the couple, thinking about the ugly message on the wall. The last two letters appeared wiggly, as if rushed. The third letter might be incomplete, maybe intended as "U," "O" or "D."

Was the signature meant to be "God," the work of a David Koresh type? If so, why periods after the "G" and "O"?

As the women waited, saying little, both watched the pastor's still form. His breathing remained shallow. Juanita now noticed a skinned patch on his chin and a cut above his eye. Her gaze dropped to his hand, where gray smudges darkened knuckles and wrist. A glance at her own fingertips showed similar traces. She sniffed her hand, but detected no aroma.

"What was Rev. Asher doing over here this time of night?" she asked.

"We'd gone to bed," Mariette said, one hand pressing the gauze to her husband's face, the other stroking a dark cowlick at his crown. He was mid-thirtyish, slightly younger than Juanita. "Our bedroom window was open a crack, and Ferris thought he heard noises over here. I said it was just the wind, but he's such a mother hen about the church." Her hand left the cowlick and rubbed her own forehead as if to wipe away the memory.

Juanita gave her arm a comforting pat. "Hang on, help should arrive soon. I saw three guys run out of the church. They must've been spraying that *thing* on the wall and your husband surprised them."

Mariette didn't reply.

"Does that flashlight over there belong to you?"

"What? N-no, I–don't recognize it. Ours is a small plastic one. Ferris may not have brought it—the street lamp's pretty bright in front, and the vestibule overhead turns on just inside . . ."

"I guess the vandals dropped it." Juanita stretched one leg to ease a cramp. "Do you know what that message means, or who the men might've been?"

"No. Where *is* that ambulance?"

"Surely it won't be much longer. How about the signature, G.O.L? Mean anything to you?"

"No." The golden head lowered. Mariette sobbed.

The ambulance came, then Lieutenant Wayne Cleary and a younger policeman, Jesse Black. The sight of Wayne's ruddy face cheered Juanita but surprised her too, since he usually worked days. Built like a piece of earth-moving equipment, Wayne dwarfed her size 16—part of what attracted her to him, she supposed. To the uninitiated, he appeared big and dumb. The "big" part was right.

He told Jesse to check around outside the church and directed the women to seats away from the pulpit area. Juanita sat with her arm around Mariette's shoulders, murmuring soothing phrases. Wayne snapped photos of the scene and conferred with emergency medical technicians working over the victim, then talked with Mariette while Juanita consumed nervous energy pacing the aisle.

Soon the EMTs wheeled Asher out on a gurney, Mariette following. Juanita joined Wayne in a rear pew, kicking off her low-heeled walking pumps.

"You okay, babe?" he asked.

His solicitous smile and clean-musky scent acted as balm to her nerves. She relaxed against the hard seatback, feeling the fatigue of released tension.

"Yeah. The bad guys ran. Probably left skid marks."

"Beauty like yours can fluster a fellow." Wayne poised a pen. "Tell me what happened."

Juanita told how her tranquil evening walk had changed to

a horror movie, except the heroine had untypically emerged unscathed. As she talked, details that had blurred at the time came into focus. She described the smallest man, who had exited the church first and halted on seeing her.

"I'd guess Teeny Guy was third in command. The way his feet were skittering, he wanted to be somewhere—anywhere—else. I could relate.

"The second guy out, the gung-ho one, was tall, muscular, an athlete maybe." She shivered, recalling the man towering over her, his head a silken post behind a nylon stocking, his powerful biceps flexed under a sable sweater.

"Luckily for me, Paunchy Guy must've been in charge. He called off Athletic Guy." Juanita described the heavy-set third man's pursuit of his eager cohort, stumpy thighs working like pistons, stubby hand grabbing at knitwear. "After they left," she continued matter-of-factly, "I heard moans and came into the church to check them out."

Wayne's mouth pursed disapprovingly. "What if another perp had been inside here?"

"I came armed." Juanita indicated the mace. "When Asher wakes up, I bet he'll agree I did right." She repeated Mariette's statement about hearing noises after they had retired.

Wayne nodded. "Yeah, she mentioned that."

"He must've flipped on the foyer light as he came in. Probably thought it was just kids messing in here, so didn't bother going to the office to turn on the sanctuary lights."

"Thanks for the reconstruction. I could never have figured that out myself."

Wayne's sarcasm annoyed her. She had meant well.

"How come you were walking home alone late at night?"

That again. It was true Wyndham had changed since Juanita had left just after high school, also that on moving back from Los Angeles she had relaxed her big-city alertness. But he could still lighten up.

"I worked late on a report for the library board. The chairman's Stickler Simon." At Wayne's blank look, she explained. "You're new enough in town you may not have encountered him. He's a CPA and the town fussbudget. When Simon Simms is involved in something, you can't take shortcuts or lump lots of expenses together under 'Miscellaneous.'" Juanita sniffed, pushed back her short dark hair. "Though everyone except accountants and the IRS knows that's where most belong."

"You walked to the library this morning? Seems like you'd have driven, knowing you'd be working late."

"I'd forgotten the report was due tomorrow, and in nice weather I hate getting the car out for just a five-block trip."

"Did you move or touch anything in here before I came?"

As she contemplated the solemn, "official" Wayne, Juanita's mind wandered irrelevantly to a time they had been kissing on her couch. His sandy hair tickling her temple, the surprisingly delicate touch of his lips.

Touch— Her thoughts leapt back to the present. "I handled the flashlight and felt of Asher's wrist."

"Describe those three again. As much detail as you can, please."

Juanita did, noting their dark sweaters, slacks and caps, the grotesqueness of A.G.'s stocking-clad features, the facial disguises of the other two.

"Teeny Guy wore a ski mask, purple and—yellow, I think."

"Tasteful."

"The heavy one had on makeup of some kind—oh, I bet that's what was on Asher. See." She displayed the smears on her hand. "Only it looked darker on the guy's face."

"Hm-m-m." Wayne's pen beat the paper staccato-fashion. "I noticed that on the preacher's knuckles. The military and hunters use it." He scribbled a note. "Camouflage makeup, pantyhose, ski mask. All from the Terrorist Tom Collection."

"The look worked for them. It made a statement."

"Anyone walk with a limp? Any distinguishing marks?"

She visualized the three again. "They wore gloves."

"Figures. Anything else?"

"No-o-o. Wait—when they spoke . . ." She summoned an audio memory of P.G.'s words: "No! Run!" and "I said run!" A generic male voice. Then A.G.'s throaty sounds: "Get her!" and "Don't wimp out now!"

Juanita clutched Wayne's arm. "Athletic Guy's voice seemed familiar. Deep, powerful, sort of husky. Bet I'd recognize it if I heard it again."

"Good, that could help." He flipped a page. "Though not as much as if you'd seen his face."

"Right. Next time I see hoods flee a crime scene, I'll insist on checking I.D."

Wayne chucked her under the chin. "Thanks, Juanita, you've been a big help." He mentioned details that would not be released to the media, including the vandals' appearance, and warned her not to mention them. Then he closed his book, glanced around to make sure they were alone and kissed her.

"Sure you're all right, babe? Kind of a jolt, was it?" His tone was only half-teasing.

"I'm okay. Think Asher'll be?"

"Hard to tell about head wounds. But he's young and healthy, which may help. Hope so. He's a good guy."

Juanita thought about what she knew of the minister. A mild man liberal on social issues, he had a degree from Yale Divinity School, making him an oddity in Wyndham, where ministers generally attended regional sectarian seminaries or none at all. The Ashers had come three years ago and entered enthusiastically into town life. Besides shepherding his flock, Ferris worked on civic projects and umpired Little League games, somehow keeping cool in the face of irate parents' name-calling. He was a jogger, waving and smiling at people he passed.

"What do you make of that ugliness on the wall?" she said, rubbing the broad back of Wayne's neck. "Who's 'G.O.L'?"

"Beats me."

"Suppose some outfit like the K.K.K. or the Skinheads has started up here?"

"We have to treat it as a possible hate crime, but the message and swastika could be a cover. Asher might've just preached against someone's favorite sin."

Juanita recalled times she had heard the victim speak. Nothing terribly controversial—he mentioned tolerance a lot. She supposed with old bigotries gaining new respectability, even "live and let live" was a radical idea to some. She couldn't claim to be an expert on Asher, however, being what ministers derogatorily called a "church fly." Flitting between congregations made for variety and helped her keep up on town happenings.

As a door creaked behind them, she released Wayne's neck. Jesse entered and reported finding the escapees' route through the brush, marked by broken twigs and disarranged vines. He showed Wayne fibers of a navy sweater he had found caught on a bush. Juanita said she didn't recall which man had worn blue, only that Athletic Guy had been in black.

Wayne asked Jesse to take her home while he looked around more. She started to argue, but it occurred to her A.G. might be lying in wait somewhere to silence the witness. So when Jesse opened the squad car door, she crawled in without protest. He drove through the familiar neighborhood of modest one- and two-story frame houses surrounded by lush evergreens and old winter-bare oaks, walked her to her front door and waited courteously while she unlocked it and made sure things were okay inside. She thanked him, and he left.

Scratching and whining sounds from the back of the house

told Juanita Rip had heard her arrive. She tossed her purse on a wing chair in the spacious living room, went to open the kitchen door and let in the collie-type mongrel who greeted her with eager face and swishing tail. Closing the door, she knelt and threw her arms around his neck.

"Something awful happened tonight, Rip," she crooned. "A good man got badly hurt. And I was scared. I wouldn't admit that to everybody, but you understand, don't you?"

When the gaunt young stray had come to Juanita's house a year ago, his timid manner and soft brown eyes had won her heart. Even now, he remained tentative and unsure around most people, though he would bark fiercely at postmen and trash collectors through a shielding windowpane. A fan of irony, Juanita had named him Jack the Ripper.

After feeding Rip and supplementing her vending-machine supper with cereal, eaten standing at the butcher-block counter in her kitchen, she changed from her tailored blouse and skirt into the "granny gown" she liked on cool nights. She locked the house with care and was turning out living-room lights when a vehicle stopped in front of her house. A door opened, then softly closed. Rip, dozing on his favorite rug in front of the bay window, cocked an ear.

Panic gripped Juanita. Had Asher's attackers come to get her? Looking for a weapon, she grabbed a floral-patterned umbrella from a holder by the door. It would have to do.

Footsteps mounted the porch. A low knock sounded.

Was it A.G., trying to get her to open up? Juanita waited, brandishing the parasol and silently blessing Wayne for having browbeaten her into installing a deadbolt lock. Then she realized Athletic Guy could break a window and crawl through. It would make noise, maybe waken a neighbor, but he could probably kill her and be gone before help came.

Perhaps seeing the dog would scare him off.

Sure. Or possibly A.G. would laugh himself to death at

sight of Rip slinking away from the action.

Juanita ran to the dining room, the canine right behind, and paused there, fidgeting.

"What now?" she murmured. "Go out the back? Slip down the alley? Hide in the garage?"

"Juanita, you up?"

Wayne's voice. Juanita ran to the living room, yanked back the deadbolt, wrenched the door open and hugged him. He flinched, plucked the sunshade crook from his armpit.

"Expecting a shower in the living room?"

"Umbrellas have other uses. Like protecting one's virtue."

"More likelihood of a shower in the living room, isn't there?"

She whacked him with the parasol. Rip, evidently deciding this was a new game, scratched at Wayne's pant leg.

"Hey! Just making sure you got home okay, babe."

"Jesse's a very efficient young man," she said stiffly.

"Good. Well, I'm still on duty—we're short-handed with this flu bug. Sure you're all right?"

"Absolutely. But I appreciate the concern, Lieutenant." Melting before his sideways grin, she hugged his neck. "I am fine, really. Thanks for checking on me, love."

"Part of the service. By the way, that's a fetching negligee." He kissed her, scratched Rip's ears and left.

Juanita lay awake much of the night, brain churning with thoughts about the attack on the minister. It seemed more than a prank gone wrong. But what—and who—lay behind it?

Chapter Two

Pirates chased each other off bowsprits and evil elves sprang from treetops in Juanita's dreams when she finally slept. Tuesday morning, logy-headed and half an hour late after failing to set an alarm, she stumbled through the massive door of Wyndham Public Library into the main reading room.

"Hello!" two voices chorused from stools inside the check-stand.

Juanita mentally chalked a mark on the wall. Her assistants seldom were in sync about anything.

Mavis Ralston stared pointedly at the wall clock, but leaned over to open the counter gate, a rare gesture of good will. Juanita entered the oval cubicle, took a stool between her colleagues' and fielded questions about the church incident that had been reported on morning news broadcasts. As they talked, workaholic Mavis went on substituting new magazines for old in plastic covers. Calvin Meador—Meador as he preferred—being less addicted to toil ceased checking in books from the outside bin and listened, undisguised awe in his doughy face.

"You went on in the church after seeing those guys come out? Pretty brave, Juanita."

"Dumb's more like it." Speaking *sotto voce*, Mavis could barely be heard. But she went on at conversational level. "Always thought Asher an odd duck for a preacher."

"How do you mean?"

"Different." Mavis nodded sagely. "Re-e-e-eal different."

"He seems like a nice man."

"Didn't say he wasn't."

"Then what's your point?"

"Touchy." Even in undertone, the word was clear.

Juanita briefly indulged in her favorite fantasy, imaginative ways to do in her second in command. Dunking Mavis in a vat of molten lead sounded fun, though infecting her with flesh-eating bacteria had real possibilities. If only Mavis weren't such a tireless worker.

Returning to reality, Juanita flipped through morning mail, pitched three envelopes in the trash and started to carry the rest to her office off the reading room. Meador stopped her, asking how big the vandals were.

"One was small and wiry," she said, "one well-built, probably works out. The third was heavy-set, about—your size."

She had hesitated not because she suspected her male helper had been one of the three masked men—though mercurial, Meador in all moods rivaled Gandhi for gentleness—but because of abruptly realizing how many males she must know who fit one of those descriptions. P.G.'s voice had been unremarkable—so was Meador's—but the idea that the latter could have been part of that trio was ludicrous.

Mavis glanced up from a film-covered *Good Housekeeping*, gray eyes asparkle with renewed interest. "So what's the story, Meador? Where were you last night about eleven?"

They were opposites in nearly every sense, Juanita often thought. Meador was a pillowy twenty-something, Mavis fifty and thin as a tomato stake. She was also less moody than he, being nearly always bad-tempered. She had worked at the library three years, ever since the last of a large brood left home. His arrival a year ago had given her new reason to live, tormenting him. Juanita's suggestions he ignore her gibes had so far gone unheeded.

When Meador had applied, Juanita had asked bluntly why he would work for what a small-town library could pay, when at his age and with some college he could do better.

"Tried other things," he said with a disarming smile. "Selling insurance, writing ad copy, managing a fast-food restaurant. Too stressful. Doctor said find something slower."

Charmed despite hearing her chosen life's work dismissed as "something slower," Juanita had hired him.

"Home in bed," he growled now, glowering at a circulation slip. "How about you?"

"Home," Mavis said, her chin sharp as a gravedigger's spade. "But I don't need an alibi. You do."

"Do not."

"Do too."

"Can it, you two. I can't take your nonsense today." Juanita escaped to her cluttered office, where she saw more volleys had been fired in her assistants' months-long Quote War. The upper of two new slips of paper, joining dozens already dotting one wall, said in Meador's bold script:

There is nothing more frightening than active ignorance.
—Goethe, *Spruche in Prosa*

The one below, in Mavis' precise printing, read:

It is better to know nothing than to know what ain't so.
—H. W. Shaw ("Josh Billings"), *Proverb*

Juanita sighed, hoping *Bartlett's Familiar Quotations* didn't contain many entries for "ignorance," so this skirmish wouldn't last long. She chewed antacid tablets, chasing them with water from a small refrigerator under the worktable.

The phone rang. Juanita answered. Vivian Mathiesen, reporter for *The Wyndham Daily News*, rasped in cigarette-roughened tones, "I only covered a brouhaha at city council meeting last night. Sounds tame compared to your evening."

"At least my villains wore masks."

"Something in that. Gory details, please."

"Surely you got those from the police."

"The dry facts. No color."

Juanita answered Vivian's questions, omitting information Wayne had asked her to keep quiet. When she hung up, she sat slumped at the computer, wondering if she absolutely had to stay at work today. Yes, she did. Besides doing several book orders, she had to check the committee report and have Meador deliver it to Simms's office.

The phone interview and her colleagues' queries proved to be only warm-ups. Between book orders, she dealt with questions from townspeople drawn by her new celebrity. They speculated on the culprits' identity, waxed indignant over the sanctuary's violation and indulged in plain thrill-seeking.

"*Shocking*," said Estelle Pugh, when she happened to catch Juanita in one of her trips out to the circulation desk. Banker's wife, society leader and one of Juanita's least favorite people, rangy horse-faced Estelle had as usual "dressed" for the day, her taupe jacket-dress and matching heels in stark contrast to the jeans and sneakers of most patrons. "People will *never* again worship there without recalling what *happened*. We need more *policemen* on the *streets*. When something like *that* can happen in a *church*, what's the world *coming* to?"

Wayne's response would have been, "Where were you during the last fight over the police budget, Estelle?"

Juanita said, "There's precedent, unfortunately. Ever hear of church bombings and burnings?"

"Oh, out *there*." Estelle's flung-up fingers dismissed the world beyond Wyndham. "Such things don't happen *here*."

"It seems they *do*. Last *night* jarred some *smugness* out of *me*."

If Estelle noticed Juanita's mockery, she gave no sign. "Why in the *world* did you go *inside* the church, Miss Wills? That seems *foolhardy* to *me*."

Mavis murmured agreement. At least Juanita thought so.

After Estelle left, Juanita checked out a Colleen McCullough novel for Eva Brompton, a member of Wyndham United Methodist Church. She asked if Eva knew any more of Asher's condition, which reports had given as critical.

"Still unconscious." A frown clouded Eva's plumply pretty face. "Think I'll drop by the hospital this afternoon. Mariette might like company."

"Were you in church last Sunday, Eva? Did Rev. Asher say anything that might've set this off?"

Eva propped a fleshy elbow on the counter and cupped her chin in her hand. "Now you mention it, he did seem different. He was on one of his favorite themes, respecting others' beliefs even when we don't agree with them. But his tone Sunday was unusual. Almost—angry."

"Angry."

"He said we each have a conscience for a reason, and that those who try to make others violate their consciences incur the 'wrath of God.'" Eva chuckled. "I'd never heard him use that phrase before."

"Suppose he had someone specific in mind?"

Eva shrugged gingham-clad shoulders. "Possible, I guess. If so, he didn't say who."

Doug Darrow, high school history teacher and Vietnam veteran, dropped by on his lunch hour. With his wavy sandy hair and strapping build, Doug was considered a "catch" by many Wyndham women. Juanita had had a soft spot for him herself ever since his older-kid shenanigans on a jungle gym had nearly decapitated her when she was eight. The teacher winked a merry brown eye and laid two Civil War tomes on the counter.

"I hear Library Lady galloped to the preacher's rescue last night."

Noting the similarity of Doug's form to Athletic Guy's,

Juanita shivered. His voice was deep, but less gravelly than A.G.'s. However, voices could vary with their owners' emotions, she remembered uncomfortably.

Might as well suspect Meador. But crazy idea or not, she decided to see if Doug had an alibi for last night. "Someone had to protect the town while you big strong men cowered at home." She pointed a scanner at his library card. "Or were you out romancing your latest conquest last evening?"

He batted long eyelashes. "Conquest? You're sexy when you talk Victorian, Juanita. Actually, I had company."

The front door opened and admitted a man of military bearing, his short dark hair salted with white. Juanita tensed, glanced at Doug, whose grin had vanished.

"Greetings, Miss Wills." Earl Trevethan's own smile faded. "Darrow."

"Trevethan."

The older man had moved to Wyndham on retirement from the army a few years ago, apparently seeking some ideal of small-town life. Single and gregarious, Trevethan could be found at every community event from community-college ball game to Kiwanis Pancake Day fund-raiser. If the topic existed on which the two veterans agreed, they didn't seem to have found it.

Trevethan's intense dark eyes focused on Juanita. "Hear you scuffled with some felons last night, Miss Wills."

She mentally noted his body type and voice—A.G.'s, almost to the letter. Madness, she scolded herself, imagining every man she saw had been one of the church vandals.

"Hardly. I saw them is all."

"Strange stuff they sprayed on the wall."

"Where'd you hear about that?" Wayne had told her not to mention the message's contents.

"Don't recall. Couple different people told me, I think. 'G.O.L.' must be whoever paid the masked guys to play that joke on Asher."

Doug snorted. "A bunch of modern Nazis trying to intimidate folks into buying their brand of warped thinking is no joke."

He wrenched his shoulders back in parody of Trevethan's posture, his drab military jacket a counterpoint to the other's maroon windbreaker. The paradox of their usual garb—the pacifist in government-issue, the "regular army" man in civvies—had always intrigued Juanita.

"Give it a rest, Darrow. You bleeding hearts see conspiracy everywhere."

Juanita tried a diversion. "What would you guess 'G.O.L.' stands for, Doug?"

"Garrulous Old Lawyers? Goofy Oleaginous Libertines? No telling." A thought seemed to strike him. "You weren't by any chance one of those guys, Trevethan? Seems a cowardly enough thing to be up your alley."

"I'll match battle scars with you any day, you cringing piece of shit."

"That's enough," Juanita said sternly. "This is a library, though people seem to be confusing it with a nursery school today."

"You were there last night," Doug insisted. "I notice you didn't deny that part."

Trevethan's next words dripped icicles. "I don't owe you any answers, Darrow, but I happen to have been at city council meeting. Yourself?"

"At home, with friends."

"Care to mention their names?"

"Not to you."

"This is ridiculous," said Juanita. "Stop it now, or I'll bar you both from the library."

Doug had the grace to look sheepish. "Nice seeing you, Juanita. I got a class." He took his books and left.

"Nut case." Trevethan stalked toward the periodicals rack at one end of the large reading room.

After eating a taco salad Meador brought back for her from his fast-food lunch, Juanita decided she needed fresh air. She strolled downtown, jacketed against the lingering effects of an early-morning cold front.

Wyndham had managed to keep its city center more active than those of many towns by junking parking meters, refurbishing shop facades, planting trees and flowers and offering activities to encourage foot traffic. Next month, there was to be a family fun night with contests, magicians and a puppet show. Nonetheless, a sizeable shopping center planned for the west edge of town had downtown merchants worried.

She was passing a computer store on Main when she recalled needing a printer cartridge. She went in and prowled among chest-high shelf units of office supplies, picking up floppy disks and paper clips and the cartridge, then carried her choices to a currently unmanned counter dividing the supplies section from a repair shop at the rear. The lone clerk stood by a shelf of software talking to a customer.

As Juanita waited, someone spoke in the repair shop. A husky voice. Familiar. A shudder went through her.

But from that distance she couldn't be positive. Seeing the clerk was still occupied, Juanita circled the counter and crept near the open door.

"I promised this PC today," a second voice said.

"Then *unpromise* it." The first speaker.

Juanita's knees buckled. She caught herself against the door frame.

Taking two deep breaths, she felt steady enough to edge backwards. Her foot struck the leg of a table behind the counter, sending a stack of continuous paper slithering floorward. Page after perforated page slid by before her grabbing fingers stopped the flow.

At the sounds, a man's head, dark hair in a burr cut, poked around the door facing. A tall, trim-waisted, wide-shouldered body followed.

"Help you?" The cold blue eyes narrowed as if their owner was trying to place her.

Juanita's chest tightened, her mouth felt dry as old corn husks. "S-s-sorry. I was—looking at—this printer." Corralling the jumbled paper with one hand, she pointed with the other to an appliance on the table. "I'm thinking about getting one like it."

The man disappeared into the repair shop again. The female clerk joined Juanita and cheerfully restacked the paper. Juanita paid for her items by credit card, signed the bill with shaking hands, took her purchases and left. She walked a block to a small park, where she collapsed onto a bench.

No mistaking that combination of guttural speech and muscular physique. The previous evening the voice had issued from behind a nylon stocking.

Chapter Three

". . . found him, Wayne—the voice—the build—he's it!"

Juanita hunched at her desk, babbling into the phone, her still-icy fingers cradling the pack of floppy disks. She had taken a few minutes to collect herself, hurried back to the library, flung the barest of hellos at Mavis and shut herself inside the office. Now she could almost feel her assistant's inquisitive eyes boring laser-like through the door panels.

"Slow down, babe," Wayne drawled. Juanita heard his chair creak, then a sipping sound. He would be leaning back, feet on desk, guzzling coffee. "You found who?"

"The masked man. I ran into him today—well, not literally—but I saw him, Wayne, heard him. . . ."

More squeaking, Wayne abruptly sitting up. His voice grew alert. "You saying you saw one of the guys from the church? The ones who beat up the preacher?"

"Who else?" Indignation steadied Juanita's words. "How many masked men are you currently hunting for? I can identify one of them."

"Great! But how can you be sure it's the same fellow?"

"He wore an 'I assaulted Ferris Asher' tee-shirt. Honestly, Wayne. I recognized his voice, of course."

"Okay, okay. Where'd you—wait, I'll swing by the library and you can tell me about it."

"Don't let me take you away from catching school-zone speeders or anything really important."

"No problem. I already gave out today's quota of tickets."

Wayne arrived minutes later, his bulk impressive even in the big reading room as he sauntered past the checkout desk.

"Lieutenant Cleary," said a surprised Mavis. "To what do we owe the honor of seeing you this time of day?" Her nose was fairly quivering with curiosity, Juanita noted through the open office door.

"Finally got the goods on your boss." Wayne gave a conspiratorial wink. "Once she's in the slammer, you'll take over."

Entering the office and shutting the door, he gave Juanita a big hug. Then he pushed aside a stack of papers on the worktable, laid his notebook open and sat.

"Okay, babe, let's have it."

Fidgeting with returned excitement, Juanita told of her encounter with the computer repairman.

"It was the same voice, Wayne—deep, raspy, forceful. The body was right too, tall and well muscled."

"You get his name?"

As Juanita recalled the man in the repair-shop doorway, icy blue eyes staring her up and down, she trembled again. Had he recognized her too? He would certainly know her name by now, if he hadn't earlier, because media reports had carried it.

"He wore a tan uniform shirt, but I don't recall a name imprint. Might've been too dumbfounded to notice, though."

"That's okay. Your description can't fit many who work there." Wayne eyed her keenly. "Shook you up a bit?"

"It shows?"

"You're as hard to read as a stadium scoreboard. We'll catch them, babe. When this guy knows you've I.D.'d him, he may give up his buddies too."

"You really think so?"

Wayne shrugged.

"When the Pope teaches tap-dancing in the Sistine Chapel?"

"Maybe. But people can surprise you."

"How's the investigation going so far?"

Wayne hesitated. It was a question he hated, he had often told Juanita. To her surprise, he answered.

"Not great. The church's neighbors are mostly elderly folk, in bed by eleven, and nobody saw or heard anything. The spray can's a stock item from K-Mart. No fingerprints on it, of course."

"Any luck with the sweater fragment? Or the flashlight?"

"So far, no."

She mentioned theories she had heard from townspeople, including Trevethan's that someone had hired the masked men to play a joke on the minister.

"Possible. Strange sort of prank, though."

"But Doug Darrow's convinced they were part of a K.K.K.-type group Asher somehow ran afoul of."

Wayne smiled humorlessly. "Given the message on the sanctuary wall, that's no stretch. Even we simple policemen see that possibility."

Juanita managed to keep her mouth shut.

"But as I said," he went on, "the message could be a blind. The real motive may be something personal." He jotted a note in the book. "Darrow, you say? He's at the high school, isn't he?"

She gazed at him in alarm. "Don't hassle Doug, Wayne. Worrying about the right wing is what he does—like Trevethan sees Communists everywhere, Soviet collapse or no. They balance each other out."

After Wayne left, Juanita sat a few minutes reliving the scary encounter. At last she calmed, called up the library report on her computer and started checking figures. Mavis meandered in and began casually leafing through a self-help manual awaiting cataloguing.

"You calling in the police about all the non-returns?"

"Wayne didn't come about overdue books."

"Then what was the cloak-and-dagger stuff about?"

"You mean closing the door? We didn't want to scandalize you, Mavis. You probably don't approve of people making out during working hours."

"Don't tell me, then," Mavis said with a dark look. "Too

bad those guys didn't beat you up too." She flounced out and returned to the circulation desk.

Juanita could relate to her colleague's curiosity, but Mavis had been known to use ferreted-out information against others, whereas she herself liked knowing secrets just to know them. For a moment, Juanita indulged her fantasy. She could dunk Mavis in boiling paraffin, then light the giant candle thus produced. Satisfying.

The evening paper carried Vivian's story:

LOCAL MINISTER HURT;
CHURCH VANDALIZED
by Vivian Mathiesen

Rev. Ferris Asher sustained a severe head injury last night when he apparently surprised vandals in the act of desecrating the Wyndham United Methodist Church sanctuary.

Asher, the church's pastor, remains unconscious and in serious condition today at Rochester Memorial Hospital.

Epithets had been spray-painted on a sanctuary wall, but it was unclear whether the minister himself was their target.

The vandals' motive and identity are also unknown.

Authorities ask that anyone having relevant information contact Wyndham Police.

Local librarian Juanita Wills came to Asher's aid after hearing sounds in the church and seeing three men run out. The incident occurred about 11 p.m. Monday, as Wills was walking past the church after working late at the library.

"I was plenty scared when I saw them run out," she told this reporter. "Especially when one started toward me. But another called him back and they ran away."

Wills entered the building after hearing groans from inside the building. She found Asher lying on the floor near the podium and phoned 911 from the parsonage next door.

"We don't recommend citizens take risks like Miss Wills did," said Police Lt. Wayne Cleary, who investigated. "Another perpetrator could have been inside the church. But this time she may have saved a man's life."

Mrs. Mariette Asher, the victim's wife, reported her husband had gone to the church to check on noises he heard after the couple went to bed. The Ashers' bedroom window faces the church and was open.

The church's front door had been locked earlier that evening, but Cleary noted the lock is a relatively simple type to open.

"Great," Juanita groaned aloud after reading the account. Now the two or three people in Wyndham who haven't yet asked me about this, will."

Chapter Four

Floodlit Merriam Hall rose pale and majestic atop a hill at the center of Wyndham Community College as Juanita climbed its long flight of steps Tuesday evening. She had considered skipping her weekly Books meeting after dealing with curious people all day, but liked to support the few cultural opportunities in town.

A less high-minded reason for attending was that Eva Brompton, arguably the area's best cook, would be taking her turn at providing refreshments. Juanita had eaten a light supper in anticipation.

She entered the classroom where Books met. Some fifteen people milled about, sat at long tables placed in a crescent facing the teacher's desk or stood near a refreshments table by the door. Aromas of coffee and homemade cookies overlaid an odor of chalk dust. At Juanita's approach, Willard Pugh set down his cup, poured another from a decaf urn and handed it to her. She thanked him and heaped a plate with hazelnut shortbread and coconut macaroons.

"So, Miss Wills, you're the hero of the hour." A diminutive man with chubby cheeks and rimless glasses, Pugh looked especially unimpressive beside his imposing wife in her omnipresent high heels. But he exuded the confidence of a small-town banker with yea-nay power over the locals' lives.

"I just happened to be passing the church at the right time." Juanita bit into a nutty confection, her eyes closing in ecstasy.

"False *modesty* has *never* been one of *your* faults, Miss Wills," Estelle Pugh said, brushing imaginary lint from her ivory wool suit. "No *telling* when the pastor would have gotten *medical* attention if *you* hadn't *found* him."

"Probably saved his life," agreed Cyril Brompton, Eva's

husband and owner of the local abstract company. Cyril's potbellied shape, twinkling green eyes and large balding head always made Juanita think of a yard gnome. "Even if you did go inside out of sheer nosiness."

"It was brave of you, though, to enter that dark sanctuary alone, Miss Wills," Pugh said. "What if another vandal had been lurking in there?" His hand jiggled, sloshing coffee that barely missed his wife's pale skirt. "Sorry. Clumsy of me."

"*Really*, Willard. Can't you be more *careful*?" The look Estelle gave him could have sliced fruit.

"If there'd been a lurker, I guess I'd have come out faster than I went in. Great shortbread, Eva."

"Thanks. I added extra nuts this time."

"How's Rev. Asher doing? Any late word?"

"Still unconscious when I was by the hospital around four." Eva's apple-dumpling face elongated in a frown. "Mariette's exhausted, but won't go home to rest in case he should wake up."

"I suppose you've determined the criminals' identity by now, Miss Wills," Cyril said, referring to Juanita's comment made months before during the club's discussion of Wilkie Collins' *The Moonstone*—that anyone with common sense could solve a crime. Wayne, hearing later of the remark, had not been amused.

"Your policeman friend must be thrilled to have your aid with his cases," Pugh said, his tone implying Wayne needed help from someone.

"Does Wayne consult you right away, Juanita," Doug Darrow asked impishly, "or only after he's screwed up a case?"

"This isn't a literary meeting, it's a sugar-stoked bull session," Juanita groaned.

Talk shifted to the message on the church wall.

"Whoever wrote that must be one sick individual." Cyril refilled his cup.

"Crazy, I'd say," his wife said. "'Doer of devil's work,' my eye! Ferris Asher?"

"Bigots aren't noted for their logic, Mrs. Brompton." Doug patted the olive-drab tee-shirt covering his tabletop-flat stomach. "Fantastic macaroons, by the way."

Eva beamed.

"Speaking of crazy," Earl Trevethan said with a sardonic grin, his shoulders braced under a red plaid sport shirt, "Darrow thinks there's a 'secret society' involved."

The two frequent opponents eyed each other. Lifting her eyes in a here-we-go-again expression, Eva went to speak to moderator Katherine Greer, who sat at the teacher's desk. Meador entered, tossed a bright green cardigan on a chair and helped himself to food while listening to Doug expound his paramilitary-group theory.

"A conspiracy sounds pretty far-fetched in a sleepy burg like this, Doug," Meador finally commented.

"You might be surprised what goes on in Wyndham, Meador," said Roy Boston, a corpulent man with a jovial smile and a nervous habit of rubbing his chin. "We lawyers see a side of small towns you laymen don't."

"Come on, Roy," said Cyril. "This place is so dull it barely makes the road maps."

Pugh gave Cyril a speculative smile. "I understand some people import their excitement."

Cyril reddened, glanced uneasily at Eva. She appeared absorbed in conversation with Katherine.

"Hate groups are everywhere, Meador," Doug said. "The ones that make the news are just the tip of the ice—"

"Let's begin, people." Katherine stood and clapped her hands.

The chatter ceased. Snatching two more shortbread fingers, Juanita took a chair between Doug and Meador. Trevethan pointedly sat as far from Doug as the semicircle arrangement allowed. Estelle waited like Queen Victoria for Pugh to pull out her chair, which he did with slightly too much force. Other members refilled cups, found seats and opened copies of a paperback containing *Walden* and "Civil Disobedience."

Katherine, a retired WCC English teacher, had begun the discussion circle three years ago, planning to use the "Great Books of the Western World" series published by *Encyclopedia Britannica*. But when she read a list of titles and authors at the organizational meeting, some participants protested that Plutarch, Aquinas and Shakespeare sounded dull. When it seemed the idea of a group might die aborning, Katherine agreed members could vote on reading choices.

The club's official name, Wyndham Literary Society, had never really had a chance because of Boston's comment that first lively evening: "If we're not going to read the Great Books, maybe not even good books, we'd better just call ourselves Books." The nickname had stuck.

Katherine, white-haired and dignified, her piercing blue eyes magnified behind strong lenses, summarized Henry David Thoreau's life and influence, then called for responses to the week's readings.

"Garbage." Trevethan disdainfully tossed his copy on the table. "Society couldn't function if everyone thought like Thoreau."

Boston nodded agreement. "The rule of law is a contract we make with each other. If everyone chose the statutes he wanted to obey, the world would be chaos."

"And it's not now?" Cyril quipped.

"Not all laws are good ones, Roy," Juanita objected. "What about the Jim Crow ordinances that once mandated separate drinking fountains and restrooms for black people?"

"Yeah," Doug agreed. "You saying they deserved to be obeyed, Boston?"

"Till they could be changed legally, yes." The attorney

spoke in a superior tone, a professional deigning to discuss his field with amateurs.

"If minorities had waited for legislators to change things, they'd have waited forever," Darrow snapped. "They had to force the issue with marches and sit-ins."

"Pure media manipulation," Trevethan growled. "The media knew they were being managed too, but didn't care. Hell, they loved it. When they get hold of a story they like, they don't let go!"

In Trevethan's excitement he half-rose, jarring his neighbor Pugh out of what appeared to be deep thought.

"Calm down, everyone," Katherine reprimanded. "We can disagree without being disagreeable."

Quiet reigned a moment, save for the hisses of coffee urns. Infrequent scoldings by the moderator, a former WACs sergeant, carried weight.

"So, Mr. Darrow," she went on more pleasantly, "you agree with Thoreau that a person must follow his conscience even if it conflicts with the law?"

Doug replied in the affirmative. Juanita only half heard, however. A disquieting small voice inside was whispering that something she had seen or heard here tonight related to the attack on Asher. But what? A statement? A tone or speech pattern? A manly shape?

Juanita considered the men present. Identifying the computer repairman had told her neither Doug nor Trevethan was Athletic Guy, but Boston resembled Paunchy Guy and his voice could qualify. Meador, she recalled uncomfortably, answered the description too.

Then there was Willard Pugh, the right size for Teeny Guy, the man who hadn't spoken Monday. The catch there was that she couldn't see the self-assured banker as third in command in any endeavor. As she watched him, Pugh appeared to reach some decision.

"Mr. Darrow isn't exactly consistent," he said with a grin. "As I recall, when Ollie North claimed he had to 'go above the law' in Iran-Contra, Mr. Darrow wanted to lock North up for life."

Trevethan guffawed. Doug began a retort, but peacemaker Cyril forestalled it.

"Thoreau at least lived up to his principles," the abstracter said. "He went to jail rather than pay taxes he thought were being used for unjust purposes."

"So what?" Roy Boston said, stroking his chin deliberatively. "Both slavery and the Mexican war continued. All Thoreau got for his protest was a night behind bars."

"Thanks to whoever paid his taxes for him," Pugh said, "Thoreau made out like a bandit. He got to preach his high-and-mighty ideas but take none of their consequences."

"Thoreau didn't ask anyone to pay, Willard," Juanita said. "He'd have preferred to stay in jail."

"So he said. Can we believe him?"

"The man was a *tightwad*," Estelle offered, patting her silvery gray hair. "Nothing *admirable* in *that*."

Juanita had been surprised to see Mrs. Pugh at the first Books meeting, supermarket tabloids and movie-star biographies being her reading matter of choice. But then she had realized the banker's wife considered Books just another social occasion. Estelle's contribution to the planning session had been to suggest members hear professional reviewers rather than reading selections themselves, as had a book club she'd attended as a young woman in Dallas. To Juanita's amusement and Katherine's clear relief, the proposal had gone nowhere.

"What *would* Thoreau have *done*," Estelle went on now, "if *Emerson* hadn't let him *live* on his *land*?"

Juanita suspected she had pried that bit of information out of Willard. Even using Cliff's Notes required reading.

Meador spoke. "At least Thoreau was right about people's lives getting too complex. We should all try going off alone some time and living off the land."

Sure, Juanita thought. A hermit by nature, Meador could probably handle the "alone" part. As for "living off the land," she doubted he would make it twenty-four hours without Blue Bell ice cream or Little Debbie cakes.

"He does make sense there," Trevethan conceded. "Self-reliance teaches a man what he's made of. But politically, the guy was a loon."

At Juanita's side, Doug's fist clenched.

"Easy," she murmured.

"Some of us can't go trudging around in the countryside, Meador," Boston said with a supercilious smile. "We're too busy making a living."

"Bullshit," Trevethan said. "Nobody's so important he can't take an hour out of his schedule now and then."

Boston colored. "I have plenty to do at my law office, Trevethan, without putting an oar into everyone else's business the way some do."

"And some people don't have sense enough to know when they're being helped."

Intrigued, Juanita looked from one to the other. Battles between Trevethan and Doug were old stuff, but Trevethan and Boston? Their exchange seemed more personal than a simple book discussion, she thought.

The animated debate that followed called on Katherine's referee skills. Pugh contributed wry digs at various people, with Cyril as his favored target. Juanita was reminded of an earlier evening when the banker had twitted the abstracter about having secrets. Cyril had gotten defensive, insisting that liking one's privacy didn't make one guilty of anything.

When the Thoreau discussion ended, secretary-treasurer Cyril sold copies of Machiavelli's *The Prince* for next week.

As Juanita paid, she smiled to think how many Great Books titles Katherine was managing to sneak in through skillful leading of the selection process.

Meador, Doug and Estelle drifted out the door after Cyril as he carried empty platters to the Bromptons' car. Juanita helped Eva wash and lock away coffeepots and cups, while Katherine tidied chairs. Pugh and Trevethan made no move to help, sitting comfortably while the latter extolled an anti-gun-control editorial he had read in *The Daily Oklahoman*, Oklahoma City's influential conservative newspaper. When housekeeping chores were finished, Katherine gathered several paperbacks from the desk, doused lights and shooed everyone out. Juanita held the moderator's books while she wrestled with the lock on the building's door. Atop the stack lay a cryptogram magazine.

"Oh, I love these puzzles," Juanita said.

Katherine smiled. "They're relaxing. I always carry a book of them for whenever I get a spare minute."

"You girls ought to try breaking a *tough* code," Trevethan said, "like I had to do in the army."

Pugh smiled enigmatically at Juanita.

The five walked to the parking lot, where Doug and Meador stood under a pole lamp, Meador chewing on something.

". . . up to us to defend ourselves . . ." Doug broke off at the group's approach. Taking a plastic bag printed with red Chinese characters from a pocket, he smiled mischievously and offered it. "Dried lychee nut, anyone?"

Juanita took one, the others declined. Eva and Katherine said goodnight and got into their cars. The four men watched as Juanita examined the lychee under the light. Pale brown, with a rippled surface, it was slightly smaller than a golf ball. Doug took one, crushed its thin shell, popped the contents into his mouth, chewed briefly and spat a seed onto the concrete. Following his lead, Juanita ate hers. The moist dark fruit's flavor reminded her of dried prunes.

"Tasty. Where'd you get these?"

"Asian grocery in Tulsa. First tasted them in Vietnam."

"Darrow just loved the 'gooks,'" Trevethan mocked. "Everything they ate too, fishheads and all." He climbed into a late-model gray sedan parked beside Juanita's ten-year-old blue Chevy. "Goodnight, people."

Juanita offered Meador a ride, but he said he had already accepted one from Doug. She smiled, glad her young assistant had made a friend. When she turned the key in her Chevy's ignition, the car refused to start. She tried again. Same thing. Doug offered a jump from his motor, but on the third try her car started.

As she drove home, she thought about the evening's session. Tension between Doug and Trevethan was nothing new, and some books did provoke stronger feelings than others. However, the meeting just ended had been unusually scrappy. Pugh had hinted before that he knew something embarrassing about Cyril, but tonight had practically hummed the "I've Got a Secret" theme in Brompton's ear. As for Trevethan and Boston, Juanita didn't recall their sparring so much previously.

That little voice within Juanita was still insisting she had been given some clue tonight about the church incident, some hint she was too thick to understand.

"But all those people are upstanding citizens," she said aloud. "Not the sort to be involved in anything illegal."

"Remember who populated the Klan in post-Civil War days?" came the reply.

Less than an hour after Juanita arrived home, the first anonymous phone call came.

Chapter Five

"Don't be prying into something that don't concern you, lady," the hushed voice said. "Could be dangerous."

She heard a click, then a dial tone.

Juanita raised her eyes to the ceiling. The prank had Doug Darrow written all over it, although she wouldn't put it past several other Books members either. Would she never live down that "detecting is common sense" remark?

She changed to a robe and was at the kitchen table sipping cocoa when she heard Rip snuffling outside. Then a timid knock sounded at the back door. That would be her neighbor, Bach Nguyen, who often came over evenings to practice speaking English. Juanita opened the door and found Bach on the porch, tiny and graceful in skinny jeans and tee-shirt, hands clasped demurely on abdomen.

"You have time tonight?"

"Sure, come in." Juanita calmed Rip, left him out and closed the door after the visitor. She longed to finish unwinding and go to bed, but made more cocoa instead. When the women were seated across from each other, Juanita noticed Bach's delicate face looked drawn, her dark eyes teary.

"Something wrong, Bach?"

"I scared, Juanita." A TV addict, Bach understood and pronounced English well, but as the Nguyens used Vietnamese at home her spoken English was shaky. The graceful throat worked a moment, the thin shoulders quivered.

Though scarcely older than her visitor, Juanita felt her motherly instincts aroused. She gently touched Bach's arm. "Take a deep breath. Now, what are you afraid of?"

Bach inhaled hard. "We get letter." She drew another long breath, and the story tumbled out. The Nguyens had received an unsigned note addressed to "Filthy Gooks." Bach hadn't recognized all the obscenities, but her husband Tinh, who worked at a convenience store, had. The gist had been that Vietnamese weren't wanted in Wyndham and must leave "or else." Bach asked what "or else" meant.

"It means something bad will happen if you don't do what the letter says."

She nodded as if Juanita had confirmed her fears.

"It may be an empty threat, though," Juanita added. "Sometimes people—stupid ones—think it's funny to scare others."

A tear appeared in Bach's eye, spilled down her dusky cheek. "You think this people hurt my children?"

"Hard to say, Bach. But you must take that letter to the police. It's against the law to send such things through the mail."

"Tinh throw away. He say he take care."

"What did he mean, he'd take care of it?"

Bach watched her forefinger trace a figure eight on the table's Wedgwood-blue enamel, then lifted worried eyes.

"I think he shoot."

"He has a gun?"

"Yes."

Juanita asked if she or Tinh had any idea who had sent the note. Bach shook her head.

"You think other letters come?"

"It's possible. But if you get another one, tell your husband to take it to the police. They'll try to find out who's bothering you. Tinh could get in lots of trouble if he shoots anyone, or even threatens someone with a gun."

Bach agreed, but didn't sound confident. She changed the subject to the incident at the church that Tinh's customers had talked about that day. A singsong note entered Juanita's voice as she told the story again. Bach asked about the vandals' facial disguises, seeming especially interested in the ski mask. Since some details had already leaked out, Juanita got scratch pad and pen and made a crude drawing. Her neighbor's face lit as she pointed at the paper.

"I saw!"

"You've seen a ski mask before? In a store, you mean?"

"No, in house I clean. Same." She put her slender hands together and slowly drew them apart, as if stretching a knit head covering.

"Whose house?"

"Blompton."

Juanita felt a tingle of excitement. Immediately she regretted her readiness to suspect good friends. "A ski mask in the Brompton house? What colors?"

Bach sipped her drink, pondering. "Yellow and—green?"

"You sure about the colors?"

"Yellow, sure. Green, maybe."

Bach had seen the mask at the back of a dresser drawer when she was putting away Cyril's clean socks. She'd looked at it twice since, trying to figure out its use.

"Didn't you ask Mrs. Brompton what it was for?"

"Oh, no. She think I nosy."

Juanita thoughtfully drained her cup. "Next time you clean there, why don't you make sure about the colors. But don't say anything to either of the Bromptons. Okay?"

"You think it same?"

"I'm sure it's not."

After Bach left, Juanita stared into chocolate dregs in her cup. Even if the Bromptons' mask was yellow and purple instead of yellow and green, that proved nothing. She couldn't imagine either Brompton involved in such doings. On the other hand, skiing wasn't a major sport in Oklahoma. The Nguyens' letter and church attack were probably unrelated, but together suggested an ugly undercurrent to life in Wyndham. Burglaries and bar fights were common, but intimidation? Was Boston right, that she was unaware of the town's seamier side?

Since returning home she had occasionally missed the cultural, shopping and dining opportunities available in cities, but had come to love the slow pace and neighborliness in Wyndham, even the idiosyncracies of some town residents. Sometimes she wondered if she was giving enough back. Perhaps this was a contribution she could make, to expose whoever was frightening citizens. Maybe she'd test out that theory about detecting being a matter of common sense.

Wayne mustn't know, of course.

Recalling Bach's gentle face pinched with fear, Juanita crushed the ski mask drawing into a ball, resolving that the culprit wouldn't get away with this.

But now the stains in her cup seemed to represent remnants of lost innocence. She knew the guilty party or parties just might.

Chapter Six

Meador breezed in the library door his typical five minutes late on Wednesday, cheeks pink from hurrying, round face beaming good will. He called to his colleagues seated inside the checkstand, with more alliteration than accuracy, "Marvelous matins to ye, merry maidens."

Tired from another restless night, Juanita managed a weak smile. Mavis's "Hmph" was less forceful than usual, but calling either of them "merry" struck Juanita as excessive. However, with her assistants in a state of comparative geniality, it seemed safe to leave them alone together. Issuing a few instructions, she went out to her car, which she had driven today in order to do errands.

Approaching the Chevy parked a block from the library, she noticed a lad of around ten, evidently AWOL from school, about to pass it. Impulsively she took from her purse a device Wayne had given her which could start a vehicle from up to 400 feet away, even from inside a building. She found it handy in cold weather, and also enjoyed its effect on others.

She pressed the button. The auto started, immediately this time. The headlights came on and a siren chirped. Startled, the boy glanced around and saw Juanita. She waved the remote. With a shrug, he walked on. Kids, she thought, jaded with technology.

She first stopped at Rochester Memorial Hospital, a small but up-to-date facility named for one of Wyndham's wealthier deceased citizens. In the third-floor lounge she found Mariette Asher slumped on a sofa, facing a heavily built man seated on a plastic chair. A litter of paper cups in a wastebasket reeked of stale coffee.

"The preacher hasn't waked up at all? That's a long time to stay unconscious." The visitor, who had a shock of gray hair and a wide mouth that appeared smile-proof, spoke in hushed "hospital" tones as he shifted a cowboy hat from one knee to the other.

There was something about this man, Juanita thought, something vaguely familiar. She had seen him before or heard his voice, maybe on the phone. But in what connection?

"The doctors say head wounds are unpredictable," Mariette said in a strained voice. She wore a neat French braid and a fresh-looking skirt and blouse, but lines etched around her eyes and mouth told of a long vigil. "They can't tell me when Ferris will wake up." She caught back a sob. "Or if."

The visitor looked up at Juanita's approach and nodded formally, uncertain recognition leaping into his eyes. Mariette's gaze followed his, and she smiled a welcome. He rose.

"Well, we'll all be hoping and praying for the best, Mrs. Asher. Someone else is here to see you, so I'll run along. Remember, if there's anything I can do . . ."

Mariette thanked him. With another nod to Juanita, he strode quickly out the door.

"I believe I know that gentleman," Juanita said, "but I can't place him."

"Mr. Fuller? It was nice of him to come. I hadn't met him before."

Juanita recognized the man now: Walt Fuller, superintendent of Wyndham's streets department. She had spoken with him at his city-building office last year about new curbing being laid past her house.

"Is he a friend of your husband?"

Mariette frowned. "Mr. Fuller said they knew each other from Kiwanis. Ferris has never mentioned him, though, and I thought I knew all the Kiwanians."

Juanita made a few sympathetic remarks, to which Mariette politely responded. Then silence. Juanita fidgeted with her purse strap, feeling she couldn't decently leave yet.

Recalling her resolve of the night before, she asked if Mariette had thought of anyone who might have attacked her husband.

"No." Mrs. Asher studied the hands lying palms up in her lap. "It's hard to believe anyone would want to hurt Ferris. He's such a kind, helpful man."

"That's true. How about those epithets on the church wall? Anybody ever call him such names before?"

"No."

"Had anyone threatened him?"

"No. Mr. Cleary's been asking me these same questions, but I've hardly been able to string two thoughts together for worrying."

"Your husband hadn't gotten any intimidating letters?" Juanita persisted, Bach's problem fresh in her mind. "Or phone calls?"

"I haven't seen any such letters." Mariette ran a finger over her lower lip. "As for the phone, no—oh, actually there were some calls lately that he took in his study and didn't discuss with me."

"You don't know who phoned or what about?"

"No. I assumed a church member had a personal problem."

"How many such calls?"

"Four or five. Come to think of it, they seemed to make him edgy."

"Eva Brompton noticed he was different in church last Sunday. Like he was angry, she said."

"Ye-s-s, perhaps. At the time I put it down to irritability because he was getting a cold." Mariette flexed her back, releasing tension.

"He seems such a gentle man. Hard to imagine him mad."

Mariette smiled. "He has his moments, like everyone. He's usually very controlled in the pulpit, but now and again—like a few weeks ago . . ."

"What happened then?"

"Ferris preached the fieriest sermon I've ever heard him give. He'd read this magazine article that upset him."

"What about?"

"Militia groups. He'd been concerned about them even before the Oklahoma City bombing. Some of them build up small armies, actually plan to overthrow the government."

"I know."

"This particular piece described how they recruit teenagers, appeal to young men's insecurities, their need to belong and prove they're someone." Mariette shivered. "How can people have so much hate in them, even ones who call themselves Christians?"

Juanita had no answer. Soon she left and drove to the post office, where she bought stamps and padded mailers in the main room, then went to an adjacent area that housed rental boxes and mail chutes. Cyril Brompton knelt by a wall of mailboxes, sunlight through the glass door bouncing off his gnome's head, a clutch of envelopes on the floor beside him. He was removing a package the size of a ream of paper from a mailbox on the bottom row.

"'Lo, Cyril. Your million come today?" Juanita slipped letters into the "in town" and "out of town" slots.

Cyril closed the mailbox, twirled the combination lock, piled the envelopes atop the parcel and rose.

"Not today. Yours?"

"Must be waiting for me at home."

"Ow! You turkey! That's my eye!" The high-pitched complaint came from a huge ball of energy hurtling through the door, appendages flailing in all directions. Juanita saw it consisted of three young males, pummeling each other with hands and feet. Only three?

"Boys, boys. Mom won't buy ice cream."

The lads ignored their harried-looking follower's half-hearted scolding. Yelping and grunting, they careened across the room and into Juanita. A toe kicked her shin. A fist jabbed her solar plexus. She pressed against the wall of boxes, metal hardware digging into her hip. A small shoulder broadsided Cyril. Mail spun from his arms and scattered.

As suddenly as the pint-sized tornado had arrived, it left. The woman crammed letters into a slot and gave chase.

Juanita peeled herself off the wall and bent to help Cyril. He reached for the parcel at her feet, but she got it first. The return address was a postal box, the town and state smudged, the addressee "J. Lange." Looking chagrined, Cyril retrieved his envelopes and held out a hand for the package.

"Lange?" Brows raised, Juanita handed it over.

"I'm collecting mail for a neighbor." With a hand that shook slightly, Cyril heaped letters onto the box.

"I thought I knew all your neighbors. Don't recall a Lange."

"He's a shut-in, lives a couple blocks away. I feel kinda sorry for the old guy, so I volunteered to get his mail."

Curiosity piqued, Juanita would have pursued the matter, but Cyril excused himself and hurried out.

She was back at the library, working with Mavis at the counter while Meador shelved returns, when Wayne entered and motioned her to the office. Once they were closeted alone, he gave Juanita a puzzled look.

"Babe, you sure about the I.D. of that computer guy?"

"Yes." She leaned against the shut door. "Why?"

"Well, Cooper—that's the guy's name, Gib Cooper—has an alibi for Monday. Says he and Eddie Wagoner rode around all evening. The kid backs him up."

Juanita's eyes went wide. "That was his voice, Wayne. He's built like Athletic Guy too."

Wayne searched her face, then nodded. "I believe you. For what it's worth, I thought Eddie acted kinda funny about it." He studied the floor. "I'll let the boy think it over a day or two, then question him again. If he lied, that'll give him time to reconsider conning the police."

"*If* he lied? He had to be lying."

Wayne grinned teasingly. "Don't rev your motor. If the kid's bullshitting me, I'll find it out."

Juanita mentioned what Mariette Asher had said about the phone calls and the article on militias that had upset her husband.

"That's more'n she's told me, times I've talked to her," Wayne said with a frown.

"I think she just remembered. Said she's been too worried to think straight."

"I'll speak to her again. Thanks." His hazel eyes grew tender, and he embraced her. "Come for supper tonight? I made a big beef stew that'll be even better warmed up."

"Okay, sure."

"Six-thirty? Can't make a night of it—got to go in later. We've still got several guys out."

"Okay. See you tonight."

Some weeks they saw each other in passing if at all. They had talked marriage, but neither was eager. Before moving to Wyndham, Wayne had lost his wife to her wealthy doctor-employer. Juanita had been left a young widow when her charming daredevil husband died in a skydiving accident. Though attracted to men who took risks, she was reluctant to marry another.

Willard Pugh came by over the lunch hour, his small frame dapper in a well-cut tan suit. He looked over a shelf of new arrivals, then turned to Juanita, who sat alone at the circulation desk.

"You get the latest Dick Francis yet?"

"I believe it's out. Let me check." Juanita called up a computer record, then a different one. "It's out and we've several on a waiting list. Shall I add your name to it?"

Pugh waved a hand. "It's not that important. I'll find something else."

He wandered to the stacks located off one end of the reading room, returning a while later with two books, which he laid on the counter.

"Guess I'll try Robert Ludlum. Think I'll like him?"

"He's not my taste, but he's popular." Juanita checked out a Ludlum novel, then a how-to book about crafting small furniture pieces. "You taking up woodworking, Willard?"

He grinned sheepishly. "I doubt it. But looking at Earl's projects the other evening got me interested."

"Earl Trevethan? Buy-me-a-bazooka-and-I'll-follow-you-anywhere Earl?"

"He's surprisingly talented. Get him to show you through his workshop some time. Wonderful inlaid tabletops, lovely chairs—excellent workmanship."

"Earl a woodworking hobbyist. I'd no idea."

"There's a bit more to him than shows on the surface."

"Probably true of lots of people." Juanita stacked the volumes in front of Pugh.

His watery blue eyes narrowed thoughtfully behind the rimless glasses. "I don't know, I think some folks are just what they seem. You, for instance. Or do you lead a double life, Miss Wills?"

"I can barely manage one."

Pugh seemed uncommonly talkative today, Juanita thought as she settled back on her stool. He seldom visited the library, though his downtown bank wasn't far away.

"I feel sorry for Earl," Pugh said. "He's lonely."

"Lonely? He surrounds himself with people. Never misses a ball game, school carnival or auction."

"Exactly. Because he doesn't have any real friends." Turning the books on end, Pugh tapped them on the counter. "I saw him at council meeting Monday. He always attends, sometimes makes a speech."

She nodded. So Trevethan's alibi for the evening of the church attack had been the truth. Not that it mattered, now she knew he wasn't Athletic Guy.

"He invited me to come over later to see his woodworking, but I begged off. Felt guilty about it later, so I dropped by last night after Books."

Juanita leaned on the counter. "Earl does like to make speeches. I heard him once at city council, though I seldom go myself."

"Me either. I was there Monday because of a zoning case I was interested in." Tapping the books again, Pugh gave her a speculative look. "That reminds me—remember that rezoning a while back that Ferris Asher opposed so vehemently? Earl spoke up in favor of the new zoning."

She recalled the battle, which had been lavishly reported in the local paper. "The new shopping center. Weren't you somehow involved too?"

"Not really. I just seconded what Asher said because he was right. The kids did need a park there. That shopping center'll cause a lot more traffic. Unfortunately the council didn't agree with us."

Juanita searched her memory for details of the zoning fight. "Roy Boston represented the landowner, didn't he? What was Earl's interest?"

"None, so far as I know. What he said at the time was, anybody who owns property should be able to do whatever he wants with it."

"He's against any zoning whatsoever?"

"Apparently. He almost ruined the deal for Boston, though. Earl's language got a bit extreme, made some pro-rezoning council members begin to have second thoughts."

Pugh started to leave, but Juanita called him back.

"Willard, how's the money supply at your bank?"

"Reasonably healthy. Why do you ask?"

"I may talk to you about an auto loan soon. I think I'm pushing my luck with the Chevy."

"Fine. Come down any time."

During the afternoon Mavis tried twice, unsuccessfully, to learn what Juanita and Wayne had discussed in their mysterious *tete-a-tetes*. Juanita empathized, but with Wayne already touchy, telling Mavis—or anyone—about his investigation was out. At least Meador wasn't pestering her for an explanation too. He must be off sneaking a read in the stacks, his habit at slow times.

Two quotes went up in late afternoon, first Meador's:

That there should one man die ignorant who had capacity for knowledge, this I call a tragedy.
—Thomas Carlyle, *Sartor Resartus III. iv*

Mavis answered:

There are many things of which a wise man might wish to be ignorant.
—Emerson, *Demonology*

So far, so good, Juanita thought. At this rate, they wouldn't likely draw blood.

As she counted petty cash prior to closing, she noticed Meador's ingenuous eyes glancing quizzically at her. She wondered if Mavis had told him about Wayne's unusual visits, and if her assistants had found common ground about something at last.

But she couldn't worry about them. She had gotten an idea, how she could help solve the Asher case. If only it worked.

If it didn't, the police might be getting a new case, the murder of the town librarian at the hands of one of their own.

Chapter Seven

At Center and Main, hub of Wyndham's downtown, Pugh's Fidelity National Bank stood like a granite sentry, its wide windows hooded for night. Catty-cornered in an imposing stone building that had been an opera house and was now a clothing store, a clerk turned an "open" sign to "closed." On another corner, Jim's Jewelry looked tightly shut. On the fourth, through the large window of Wyndham Drugs, people could be seen eating supper at an old-style soda fountain. Spindly branches on redbud trees lining Main Street showed a flush of color.

The town seemed much the same as when she had grown up here, Juanita reflected. Following college in Boston, with occasional trips home till after her mother died during her senior year, she had moved to California and married. On being widowed she had come back, craving a quieter life and the small-town pleasure of seeing familiar faces everywhere. Buildings had been erected and demolished in Wyndham over the years, businesses opened and closed, but the town's character hadn't greatly changed.

Two doors from the drugstore, Okemah County Abstract Company had drawn shades, but next door Juanita spied Cyril Brompton entering the yellow brick building that housed Roy Boston's law office, carrying a parcel that looked like the one addressed to J. Lange. Juanita wondered again why her asking about it had seemed to make the abstracter nervous.

A block past downtown, she pulled up to a pump at Wagoner's Service Station. As she crawled from the car, Eddie Wagoner's head and shoulders emerged from under the hood of a bright blue Fairlane. Sandy-haired, acne-marked and thin as a wand, Eddie had a typical teen's love of cars. When not busy with station work, he could often be seen tinkering with his own Ford's innards. As Juanita had hoped, he appeared to be alone, his father evidently on supper break.

"Hey, Miss Wills," he called, grinning. "What you need?"

"Hey, Eddie. Unleaded, full tank."

"You got it." He slammed the hood, wiped his hands on a rag and opened the Chevy's gas cap.

They had met years ago when his mother dragged Eddie along on her Saturday trips to clean Juanita's house. While Edith Wagoner worked, she had delivered a critical monologue about her family: Her husband Bud hadn't the get-up-and-go to move his station out near the expressway where he could make more money. Eddie was an awkward, slow kid who would never amount to more than had his father. Eddie's sister lived in another state, never called and refused to produce grandchildren. Equally uncomfortable around Edith, Juanita and Eddie hied themselves to the back yard, where they whittled crude figurines, watched ants work or pitched pennies.

Finally, Juanita got enough smarts to have Edith come Wednesdays while she was at the library, and later Edith quit to take a full-time job. Juanita had had several other cleaning women before and since, but never another as good at her job or as personally aggravating as Edith Wagoner.

Juanita felt a stirring of affection as she watched Eddie set the pump, yank a paper towel from a roll and spray window cleaner on her windshield. Getting a Dr. Pepper from an outside machine, she stood watching him, her back turned to a chilly breeze.

"How's school, Eddie?" Original, Juanita, teenagers never got asked that.

He shrugged. "Still there."

"You're a senior this year, aren't you? Got plans for after you graduate?"

"*If* I graduate. Old Lady Hawkins'll probably stop that."

He wiped the glass in big swathes.

"Hawkins—English, right? Having trouble in that subject?"

"It's the worst. She's always coming up with some stupid writing deal."

"I used to do pretty well in English. Maybe I could lend a hand."

He paused mid-wipe. "You'd help me?"

"Why not? For an old whittling buddy."

He grinned, resumed his stroke. "Okay. Thanks."

"So do you have any papers due now?"

His face fell. He applied more cleaner, flipped the towel and rubbed hard at a spot.

"That probably ain't nothing you could help with."

"Try me. What's the assignment?"

"We gotta 'interview' a person and write about them. Somebody of a different race than us, or who come here from another country." He swiped at the rearview mirror. "I don't know nobody like that. She said to call up the churches, they'd know somebody. But heck, I wouldn't know how to talk to them anyway." He aimed a kick at the front tire, as if seeing his teacher's face there.

Juanita considered. "My neighbors are from Vietnam. You could interview one of them."

"I wouldn't understand 'em, and they wouldn't understand me." Crumpling the towel, Eddie tossed it at a bucket.

"Well, you might have a problem talking to the parents, but they have a ten-year-old daughter who rattles English like she learned it in the cradle."

"A kid?" The adolescent voice went up an octave. "I really wouldn't know how to talk to a kid."

Juanita smiled. "You wouldn't have to do much talking with Lee. Ask her a question about anything, and she'll do ten minutes without pausing for breath."

He looked doubtful, but appeared to be thinking it over.

"Anyway, I know a lot about the family, so if you don't understand something Lee says, I can probably figure out what she meant. Then I'll help you with the paper."

Eddie gave Juanita a calculating glance. "You could just write one for me. I wouldn't have to see her then."

"Nope. You've got to do the interview and compose the paper as best you can, then I'll look it over and suggest ways to improve it." Juanita dropped her empty can in the trash bucket.

He hesitated, evidently decided it was the best deal he would get. "Okay, I guess."

"It'll work out, you'll see."

He took her credit card, went inside the station, then returned and handed her the card and a credit slip. As she signed the latter, she noticed he had printed his name in the "Attendant" space with the capital "E" reversed, just as he had used to do years ago. Handing the slip back, she took a deep breath and began what she had really come to say.

"There's something I want to ask you about, Eddie."

Half-turned toward the station, he swiveled to face her.

"You've probably heard I was the one who found Rev. Asher after he was beaten up in the church."

Eddie nodded, slender face expressionless.

"I heard one of those men say something that night." She watched him keenly. "The voice I heard was Gib Cooper's."

The boy's gaze dropped. He swallowed hard. Then he rallied and looked up, jaw set. "Couldn't of been Gib. He was with me that night."

"It was him, Eddie. I recognized the voice. The build was right too. I'm not mistaken." Juanita held the teen's eyes with hers, willing him to confess.

He had pluck. He shook his head, and a blush ascended the lean neck.

But she could be stubborn too. "Eddie, I've no idea why

you told the police you were with Cooper. Maybe you think you've a good reason to lie for him. But what you said isn't the truth, Eddie. You know it and I know it."

"Gib and me was together," he insisted. "Must of been somebody else at the church."

For a long minute, their eyes locked.

"Okay, Eddie," she finally said. "Maybe Cooper's forcing you to help him. But it's wrong and you know it. If you want to talk about whatever's going on—any time—give me a call."

He looked so young and pathetic, Juanita longed to cuddle him as she had years ago. "Please, Eddie," she said softly. "Let me help you."

A tear glistened in one eye, but he said nothing more. She got into her car, feeling a twinge of guilt for harassing him. Eddie was usually a truthful kid, so he must have some reason important to him to lie.

As she drove away, she glanced back. The teen, still holding the forgotten credit slip, stood tall as most men, but looked as vulnerable as on those Saturday mornings when he and Juanita had retreated from his mother's presence to her back yard.

Chapter Eight

The Chevy drove away, its old engine clattering. Ordinarily Eddie would have been mentally diagnosing its troubles and figuring how to repair it. Not this time. He stood in the station drive, transfixed with worry.

What had he gotten himself into? It had seemed simple yesterday when Gib dropped by the station, his usual breezy, confident self. Eddie had paused in changing a fan belt on an old Buick, his nostrils full of greasy-motor smell, and grinned at his unexpected visitor. Gib passed the time of day a while, casually tossing a cigarette pack from hand to hand, then gave Eddie a keen look.

"By the way, buddy, if anybody ever asks, you were with me last night. We cruised around all evening in my car. Went along Main, Center, Ash, then did all the country back roads." He winked, conspiratorially, as to an equal.

Eddie agreed, honored to be asked a favor by his hero. He did wonder why, though, also where Gib had really been Monday instead of at maneuvers. A woman must be involved, he decided. He was surprised when it was a cop who asked Gib's whereabouts Monday, but supported the alibi as promised. Unfortunately, Lieutenant Cleary didn't simply accept Eddie's statement and leave.

"Sure you don't have your nights mixed up, son? Think hard." Cleary spoke quietly and calmly, but his eyes never left the boy's.

Eddie gulped down a tremor of fear. This policeman had a five-inch height advantage, plus the chest and shoulders of a weightlifter. He could seriously hurt somebody.

"No, sir. It was Monday. We rode around all night."

"Where?"

"Oh, you know. Just around."

"Afraid I don't, son. Give me some specifics."

Recalling Gib's words, Eddie mentioned Wyndham's principal streets, then referred vaguely to country roads. The policeman tried to pin him down further.

"I don't know, sir," Eddie finally mumbled. "We drove lots of different places."

Lieutenant Cleary's hazel eyes looked more sad than mad, but Eddie guessed that with enough provocation they could scorch a person. Finally the cop left.

It had been a jolt to learn the real reason Gib needed an alibi, that a witness had identified him as one of the guys who had hurt the preacher. Till then, Eddie hadn't connected the attack with Guardians of Liberty. That meant the other two masked men had been G.O.L. members too. Eddie remembered the Major had also missed maneuvers on Monday. And somebody else, he didn't remember who.

Stirring from his reverie, Eddie entered the station and slid the credit slip into a drawer. That beating troubled him. Preachers were special people, God's chosen. His parents insisted he respect even those that weren't of the right denomination, the Church of God.

Still, as the Major said, accomplishing G.O.L.'s important goals might sometimes require doing questionable things.

Eddie sat at the desk gazing through settling twilight at a derelict building across the street. It looked as forlorn as he felt, its vacant windows staring blankly, the sign over its door dipping crazily. Even if the policeman hadn't believed him, he thought stubbornly, what could the cops do if both he and Gib stuck to the story?

Miss Wills would turn out to be the witness. She had given him cookies, played with him when he was little. She didn't like his mother either, he could tell. Now he had lied to Miss Wills too. Eddie slammed his fist into the desk, regretting it as his hand throbbed with pain.

She had even offered to help with his English, though Eddie doubted God Himself could pull him through that.

He rose and began to pace the tiny office. He hated the thought of talking to some smart-ass Chink kid, but his grade couldn't take more zeroes. If he could only make it through high school—. His mother was making noises about college, but he had news for her. By fall he would be old enough to join the army without her permission.

First he had to get past English, though. He suspected Miss Wills could be as tough as Old Lady Hawkins. At least in G.O.L. he didn't have to worry about old women backing him into a corner.

Eddie rolled his shoulders, easing tension. During training sessions and the Major's pep talks about what G.O.L. would accomplish once it got enough men and weapons, the organization seemed glamorous, powerful. However, no one had mentioned beating up on preachers or telling lies to cops. Three men against one didn't seem fair odds either. He guessed he had known some G.O.L. activities were illegal— that probably explained the secrecy surrounding meetings— but he had never imagined himself in trouble with the police.

Eddie flung himself down again, clutching his head in both hands. When he had been a kid, adults had seemed to have it made. Why did his life seem more complicated the older he got?

Chapter Nine

It had been an emotional and frustrating day, and when Juanita arrived home the mail did nothing to cheer her: ads, bills and a lyrical postcard from a friend honeymooning on France's *Cote d'Azur*. In her current mood, Juanita hoped the happy couple would choke on their *foie gras*.

She had just settled her body under the lush warm foam of a bubble bath when the telephone rang. At first, she ignored it, but realized it might be Wayne calling to change their plans. She crawled out, pulled a towel around her and dripped her way to the living room.

"If this is a pitch for switching my long-distance service," she told Rip as she snatched the receiver, "I may suggest a creative but painful use for a phone cord. Hello?"

Silence.

"Hello! Anyone there?"

"Butt out of what don't concern you, lady," came a whispery voice, "if you don't want your guts scrambled."

Click.

Juanita clutched the towel tighter, for an instant fearful. What if these calls weren't a joke? The man–she thought it was a man—had disguised his voice, yet it seemed eerily familiar.

No, it had to be a prank, one more annoying than funny.

She soaked briefly, donned sweater and slacks and brushed her short dark hair. Stowing Rip in the back yard, she drove to Wayne's apartment, located upstairs in a large house converted to four rentals. He met her dressed in jeans, sleeveless sweatshirt and an apron that featured an outline of Oklahoma with the Panhandle, his birthplace, drawn overlarge. The legend beneath the drawing read, "Kiss me—I'm a pan handler." Juanita kissed him, thrilling to the tenderness of his lips, and they went arm in arm to the kitchen.

Small but bright, the room had yellow chintz curtains, compact appliances and a narrow window overlooking a postage-stamp yard. Standing in the galley's center, Wayne could reach all the cabinets with his long arms. Juanita, who thought he looked like a too-big Alice in Wonderland there, had asked why he had chosen such a tiny place.

"Not much to clean," had been the succinct answer.

The booth at one end of the kitchen was snug even for an intimate supper, but Wayne had enhanced it with ivory cloth, yellow rose in bud vase and creamy china with abstract design in butterscotch and blue. He made a show of seating her, lit a candle in a wrought-iron holder—placed for lack of table space on a kitchen counter—and flipped off the overhead light. As the candle's flicker turned the breakfast nook to a romantic grotto, contentment surged through Juanita.

"Mm-m-m, this is almost worth the rest of today."

"That bad?"

"I can't begin to tell you." Won't, actually, she guiltily thought.

The stew tasted as good as promised, and he had made her favorite spinach-bacon salad. After some small talk, she asked how the Asher case was progressing, expecting his standard reply that he couldn't discuss an ongoing investigation. The candlelight must have affected him too, or else he needed to talk.

"Slow. Your friend Darrow claims to know nothing about a local militia. Says he just guessed there must be one because of what was written at the church."

"That's what I figured. You believe him, don't you?"

"Seemed sincere. But he may be a good liar."

She laid down her fork. "I know Doug from years back, Wayne. We used to ride the same school bus. He was a feisty kid, but not deceitful."

Wayne's eyes glowed like burnished copper in the subdued

lighting, and looked about as hard. "Are you saying you're a better judge of someone's truthfulness than I am?"

The replies that occurred to her wouldn't increase the evening's harmony. Juanita shoved a bite of roll in her mouth. Neither spoke for a few minutes.

"Darrow does admit he wears camouflage makeup for deer hunting," Wayne went on.

"So? Paunchy Guy's the one who wore that. Athletic Guy's the one built like Doug, but we now know A.G. is Cooper. I'm sure Doug's not involved."

"Darrow could've lent the makeup to a buddy, to 'Paunchy Guy' as you say. He could still know something about this."

Wayne offered her more stew. Applying Scarlett O'Hara's "Tomorrow's another day" philosophy to her diet, Juanita took another helping.

"The makeup Darrow had in his car today was blue," Wayne went on, "not gray like what was on you and Asher. But he may have it in several colors."

Uncomfortable with the emphasis on Doug, Juanita shifted the subject. "You see Mariette again?"

"Yeah. She repeated what you'd told me, but couldn't add anything more."

While he stacked dishes in the sink, Juanita carried dessert to the living room, which accommodated only a sofa, one easy chair and a coffee table. As they lolled on the couch, sipping coffee and crunching store-bought pecan sandies, Wayne returned to the case.

"I talked to a couple people in Asher's congregation who confirm he preached against hate groups a few weeks ago."

"You think there really is one around here? And that he was threatening to expose its leaders?"

"Conceivable."

"So where do you go from here?"

"Keep plodding, talk to people who know him, hope for a

break."

"You don't sound optimistic."

He kissed the top of her head. "There's lots of dead ends sometimes, but we've got a few leads to check out."

"Really?" She nestled into his shoulder. "You made it sound as if you had nothing."

"We got some calls after the story ran in the paper, primarily about people seen 'acting funny' near the church. Most tips like that are rubbish, but you never know. We'll keep an eye on Cooper, and I'll talk to the kid again. He may admit he lied."

Based on Juanita's own confrontation with Eddie, she doubted that. But she maintained discreet silence about it the rest of the evening.

Chapter Ten

On returning from Wayne's, Juanita read a Margaret Atwood novel a while, then switched off the bedside light. As she was snuggling into the covers, she realized she hadn't locked the front door.

"Shoot. Think I'll forget it tonight."

But the unlocked door nagged at her. She got up and, guided by rays from a street lamp outside, padded to the living room. She was turning the deadbolt's lever when noise erupted next door.

Thump! Glass shattered. *Thud.* Metal clinked tinnily.

Rip, lying near the bay window, growled low in his throat. Juanita yanked the drape aside in time to see a car spurt past her house, tires squalling.

A gunshot sounded. Someone yelled.

Rip rose and stood indecisively, watching Juanita as she eased the door open and peered out. Bathed in porchlight at the Nguyen home, Bach's husband Tinh held a handgun aloft and shouted in Vietnamese. Curses, Juanita felt sure. Rip slunk away toward the bedroom. She started out to ask what was going on, then recalling she wore only a nightgown went back for a robe.

Moments later she cautiously approached the Nguyen porch. Tinh still stood there, wiry and fierce in tee-shirt and jeans, lean face working with emotion, hand clutching the weapon to his side. Juanita hesitated, unsure how he would react if startled.

She was about to call out her friendly intent when Bach came outside and touched his arm. He jerked it away. Emboldened by her presence, Juanita started up the steps. An awful odor reached her nostrils.

"Ecc-ch. WHAT is THAT?"

The source appeared to be a large trash bag with holes punched in the sides. Tinh noticed it at the same time, walked over and wrenched off its plastic fastener. Beer cans and bottle shards clattered out, mingling with glass from a broken window overlooking the porch. Juanita held her nose against the stench of rotten food and animal feces. Tinh laid down the gun and retied the bag, his mouth a hard line. Then he reclaimed his weapon.

Juanita slipped an arm around Bach, felt her trembling. The sweet face looked full of fear. The women stood without speaking while Tinh carried the sack around the side of the house. On his return, they all went inside.

The Nguyen children huddled in nightclothes at the far end of the living room, five-year-old Van standing wide-eyed, a sobbing three-year-old Ngoc clinging to their older sister. Lee's usually confident face looked troubled, but she was bravely trying to comfort her brothers. Bach went to the children and hugged each, crooning in Vietnamese, then led them toward the bedrooms.

The living room furnishings consisted of two green vinyl chairs, a daybed with an iron frame and a brown plaid cover, an old TV, a floor lamp and a scarred coffee table. The family, not long in the United States, was saving every penny for a reliable car, but the room and its shabby contents always appeared scrupulously clean.

Tinh and Juanita took the chairs. Laying the gun on the coffee table, he opened a pack of king-sized cigarettes and lit one. Though thin and delicate-boned, his body had a suggestion of strength about it. Neither spoke. A few minutes later Bach returned and sat on the daybed. The three of them looked at each other.

"You need to tell the police about this," Juanita said.

"No police," Tinh snapped.

"Why not?"

He leaned forward, forearms resting on knees, the cigarette

dangling from his hand, a muscle working in one jaw. After a moment, he rose and stabbed out the smoke in an ashtray on the coffee table.

"No police," he repeated, collected his weapon and strode from the room.

When he had gone, Bach said, "My husband not trust police. In our village in Vietnam, they not good people."

"But whoever threw that mess at your house shouldn't get away with it."

"You know who do it?"

"Probably whoever sent you that letter. You have any ideas yet about who that was?"

"No. So how can police catch them?"

"They could ask people questions, maybe find out something. You have a right not to be bothered in your own home, Bach. And I hope Tinh has a license for that gun."

They talked a while longer. Bach grew calmer, but didn't promise they would heed her advice.

Returning home, Juanita locked up, climbed into bed and tried to read herself to sleep. But she couldn't concentrate on the words, her mind returning to events next door.

The car that had zipped past her house had been a light color, gray or tan, a late model sedan. She didn't know the make. There had been two occupants. She had the impression the passenger had been slightly built, perhaps younger than the driver.

Bach was right. Even if Tinh filed a report, she wouldn't make much of a witness.

But thinking about tonight and Monday at the church, Juanita felt cold fury envelop her. Both incidents had been bullying acts done by anonymous cowards. Her determination to learn what was going on in Wyndham crystallized. Perhaps she would tell Wayne tomorrow about the Nguyens' problem, whether Tinh liked it or not.

If only Eddie would tell what he must know . . . maybe

he would have a change of heart . . . confess to Wayne or to her. . . .

Finally, she slept.

Chapter Eleven

Juanita walked to work Thursday, morning sun warm on her shoulders. Greening lawns, snowy Bradford pear blossoms and buttery jonquils announced that spring was edging out winter.

A jarring note in the scenery was a clutch of campaign posters dotting fences and telephone poles, touting opponents in an upcoming special election to fill the seat of a county commissioner who had died in office. Seven candidates had announced, but the front-runners were Jesse Shipman, a "good ol' boy" who had recently retired as a rural school principal, and current city councilman Virg Piersall.

"ShipMAN is the BestMAN!" said one. "Piersall—a VOTE FOR VIRG is a vote for GOOD GOVERNMENT," said another. Knowing something of both men, Juanita considered the statements about equally untrue.

One placard new since yesterday struck a particularly nasty note. It featured a crude drawing of a nude man and wording that would make a pro football player blush, accusing Piersall of indecent acts with farm animals and young children. Though campaign publications never really deserved the name "literature," Juanita reflected, this sign hit a new low for Wyndham. Evidently someone desperately wanted Shipman to win.

She saw another of the posters during her short walk, and when she reached the library learned Meador had seen three on his longer one. Mavis, who had driven and thus missed out completely, fairly throbbed with curiosity as her colleagues discussed the scurrilous attack. If it weren't on library time, Juanita felt sure Mavis would run out immediately to hunt up a copy.

Meador joined the campaign to learn about Wayne's

secretive visits, teasing and dropping sly hints, but the more her assistants probed the more stubborn Juanita became. Finally Mavis began banging drawers, while Meador retreated into hurt silence.

Roy Boston phoned his weekly book requests, an Eisenhower biography and a Larry McMurtry novel, saying he would be by later to pick them up. Juanita noted the titles on a call slip. Earl Trevethan had been right about the attorney, she thought. Boston did exaggerate his own importance, for instance assuming the library staff had more time than he to locate his desired reading material. She asked Meador to pull Boston's choices when he shelved returns, muttering, "At least he doesn't ask us to deliver."

Juanita then set off to the library basement to check out an idea she had had during her wakeful night. The old zoning matter Willard Pugh had mentioned sounded worth pursuing as a possible motive for Asher's beating. She took a stack of back editions of *The Wyndham Daily News*, which prided itself on thorough local coverage, to a table and looked through them till she found a lengthy front-page story about the hard-fought city council battle. Roy Boston had argued for the property owner that the proposed shopping center would be the "highest and best use" of the land. Opposition led by Rev. Ferris Asher warned of danger to area children from increased traffic. He proposed the city buy the land for a park, thus for-malizing its use as a softball field and church picnic site, allowed by its owner while it lay vacant.

City leaders couldn't see spending so much for a park, and the shopping center was promoted as a producer of sales tax revenue. Not surprisingly, the rezoning carried.

Several of those most vocal—Asher, Trevethan, and Pugh—were not affected homeowners. Asher referred to Boston and his client as "money-grubbers," Boston to Asher's "bleeding heart." Trevethan's language had evidently been deemed too ripe to publish.

Noticing that the story carried Vivian Mathiesen's byline, Juanita called the paper and invited her to lunch. A deep-throated chuckle greeted the suggestion.

"What do you want to pry about now, Juanita Wills?"

No point in playing innocent with Vivian. As one who made her living being curious, Vivian didn't consider curiosity suspect, but neither was she easily fooled. Juanita admitted she wanted background on the shopping-center rezoning fight.

"Nothing to tell beyond what was in the paper," Vivian rasped, "but I wouldn't mind getting a free lunch out of you. You say the Coachman, 12:15?"

"Yes. See you then."

A little before noon Juanita left her associates still slamming and sulking, walked home for her car and drove to the burgeoning north edge of town. Wyndham's one fine restaurant occupied the former site of a fruit stand where Juanita had used to buy canning peaches for her mother. New homes, a realty office and a mini-mall now filled what had been open fields.

The Coachman's airy dining room featured subtle mauve wallpaper above paneled wainscoting and navy tablecloths set off with lilac china. Juanita liked it, but often found it too busy at lunchtimes. Fortunately, today Vivian had already arrived and gotten a table in the smoking section, where she sat with cigarette lit. The reporter was thin and hunched, with liver-spotted hands and arms, but even energetic cubs couldn't dismiss her as an over-the-hill broad.

"So why are you digging into that old zoning case?" she said when they had placed orders.

Juanita explained it had occurred to her that the rezoning fight might be connected to Rev. Asher's beating, and she had reread Vivian's account of the city council battle.

"You think the motive was revenge?"

"Maybe. Sounds like tempers ran high at that meeting."

"Very. Wayne deputizing you to help in his investigation?"

"You know better. I was just wondering."

"Yeah, right." The purply lips parted in a skeptical smile. "Well, if you've read the story, you probably know as much as I do. But if you have questions, shoot."

Juanita opened a packet of sesame wafers and chewed one, considering how to begin. "I gather Trevethan and Asher tangled especially hard, also that Earl's language got pretty abusive. Remember that?"

Vivian flicked ash from her sleeve. "Remember it? Hell, I was green with envy. I learned a few phrases to use on my editor when he butchers my copy."

"Did you get the feeling there was bad blood between him and Asher? Apart from the shopping-center business, I mean?"

"Hadn't thought about it. Earl bestowed some choice names on the Reverend, but he did on others too." She picked tobacco from her lip. "What was it he called Willard Pugh? Oh, yeah, 'fucking phony little ferret.' As good as Spiro Agnew when he got rolling."

The waiter brought their salads. Vivian stubbed out her cigarette and they dug in.

"I guess Asher stepped on toes too," Juanita said. "You think someone held a grudge over it?"

"Trevethan, you mean."

"Maybe. Or the landowner."

Vivian laughed. "Doyle Leggatt's not the type. Trevethan, though–might be. But he and Roy Boston also crossed swords, though they were arguing on the same side. Boston was trying to come across as the nice guy, a public-spirited citizen helping the town's economy. Earl got so loud and heavy-handed he almost blew the deal for Roy." She pushed away her plate. "So if you want grudges, seems to me Boston vs. Trevethan is as likely as Trevethan vs. Asher. Of course, that wouldn't explain the attack on the Reverend."

But it could be why Trevethan and Boston had been so at odds during Books meeting, Juanita thought.

Beef barley soup arrived for her, leek quiche for Vivian. They ate a moment in silence.

"Vivian, you said you were at the council meeting this past Monday?"

The reporter nodded, mouth full of quiche.

"How late did that last?"

"Eleven, 'leven-fifteen. You know those meetings. What looks like a simple suggestion provokes a brouhaha."

"I understand Willard Pugh went. Some zoning case?"

"Yeah, there were several of those. Most sailed right through. Pugh owns rental property near a lot being zoned for a video store, and asked questions about the off-street parking provided. Once he was satisfied about that, he left."

"About what time?"

Vivian raised her eyebrows. "Eight-thirty or so, I guess. Rezoning cases come first on the agenda."

"I also understand Earl Trevethan was there."

"As usual. Didn't make any speeches Monday, though."

"Roy Boston?"

"Matter of fact, he was. Represented the property owners in a couple zoning cases." Vivian explored the cracker basket, found garlic breadsticks and opened them.

"About what time did Earl and Roy leave?"

Vivian paused in munching a breadstick. "I think both stayed till the last dog died. The real squabble came late in the evening. The residents of that area the city annexed recently to the north aren't getting their services and were plenty steamed."

Though Juanita felt ninety-nine percent sure Cooper was A.G., a tiny part of her had been keeping Trevethan in reserve as an alternate. Yet if Vivian's times were correct, this made the second confirmation of his alibi. Nor could Boston have been among the minister's attackers. Pugh could have managed it easily, but she still couldn't see the self-assured banker as the uncertain Teeny Guy. If the reporter were off by half an hour or more about the adjournment time, however—even Boston and Trevethan might not be out of it.

Ridiculous, Juanita. Some imagination.

They finished their meals, and the reporter lit another cigarette. Juanita changed the subject.

"Vivian, you ever come across a guy named Gib Cooper? He works at the computer store on Main."

"Yeah, a real hunk. You two-timing Wayne with another fella?"

Juanita ignored the gibe. "So you know him?"

"Not well. I interviewed him once about a record catfish he caught at the lake. Sports editor had lots on his plate, so I covered it." She took a drag and blew it out. "Went by Cooper's house to get a picture of the prize catch. With his fish." She coughed. "Strange place."

"How do you mean, strange?"

"Oh, weapons and souvenirs he'd taken off enemy soldiers were scattered all through the living room. Scenes of Vietnam were tacked to walls, plus a photo of a Vietnamese guy he was using for knife-throwing practice. And spread on one wall was a huge map of the country, with pins indicating battle sites." Vivian narrowed her eyes against a puff of smoke. "I don't know, it's like he's still over there. Or brought the war home with him."

"They all brought it back, didn't they, one way or another?"

"I suppose." Vivian tapped her cigarette on the ashtray. "But you know, I've talked to lots of vets—had three nephews there and I've interviewed plenty. They all mention flashbacks, emotional problems, inability to get on with their lives. But this struck me as different. Downright spooky."

"You know anything more about Cooper, Viv? Like who his friends are?"

"Don't know if he has any. Wait, I saw him once at the drugstore having coffee with Earl Trevethan. Odd coincidence, isn't it? We were just talking about Earl."

"Yeah. Coincidence."

Vivian asked what her interest in Cooper was. Juanita tried being noncommittal, but the reporter smelled a story.

"Listen, Wills, I'm not dumb enough to think all those questions about where people were Monday night, and when, were idle conversation." She ground out the cigarette. "You're onto something about the Asher case, aren't you?"

Juanita smiled, innocently she hoped.

"I expect an exclusive on anything you uncover."

"Okay, except there won't be anything."

Juanita paid the bill, and they left. Vivian was getting into her tan Camry when Juanita recalled the lewd campaign poster. She asked if the reporter had seen it.

"No, but sounds like it could be grounds for a libel suit. Think I'll ask Piersall's campaign manager about it."

"I'd be interested in knowing what you find out."

Juanita returned to the library. She was stowing her purse in a desk drawer when she noticed two new quotes gracing the office wall. The one in Meador's scrawl said:

The most I can do for my friend is simply to be
his friend.
—Thoreau, *Journal*, February 7, 1841

Juanita frowned, wondering how something as uncontroversial as friendship had become part of the Quote War. She read the other slip, in Mavis's tight printing.

*It is more shameful to distrust one's friends
than to be deceived by them.*
—La Rochefoucauld, *Maxims*

She studied the slips a moment, then their meaning hit her. The combatants had found a common enemy.

Juanita Wills.

Chapter Twelve

Juanita studied the new slips of paper, thinking back over the history of the Quote War. Soon after Meador had come to work, he had begun tacking whimsical little sayings to walls and shelves in the reading room, mostly in praise of books:

A good book is the precious life-blood of a
master-spirit, embalmed and treasured up on
purpose to a life beyond life.
—John Milton, *Areopagitica*

It struck Juanita as an interesting quirk in her new underling. And who, she figured, could object to promoting reading in a library?

Her other underling, of course. Mavis pulsated indignation.

"They don't do that in other libraries," she sniffed, delivering what she clearly saw as an unassailable argument.

"It doesn't hurt anything, Mavis," Juanita said. "Several patrons have told me they like the quotes. I enjoy them myself."

Mavis said no more aloud, but her sour expression spoke volumes about Juanita's lack of professionalism. Laid-back Meador didn't argue with his counterpart, but the more she groused about the notes, the more of them went up. With each addition, Mavis informed the boss.

Then the slips began disappearing. Meador protested to his superior. Feeling like a playground monitor at a kindergarten, Juanita issued a decree.

"Mavis, quit stealing his signs. Meador, don't hang so many. Half a dozen at once—no more."

He quickly dashed off the allotted number and put them

up, Mavis glaring silently the while. The next day one paper lay on the floor below where it had hung.

"Juanita," Meador reported, "Mavis is doing it again. Taking down my quotes."

The wide-eyed innocence Mavis affected would have tipped off the most obtuse observer, but she said, "It fell. You didn't pin it up very well."

Meador clearly knew better, but reattached the note. Firmly. Modern houses should be built so well, Juanita thought. Later the sheet again lay on the floor. Meador complained, Mavis denied.

"That's it!" Juanita said, slamming shut a volume of *Books in Print*. "I ought to sentence both of you to read and write a review of *Sir Charles Grandison*. As almost no one knows—or needs to—it's a seven-volume, twenty-five-*hundred*-page eighteenth-century 'novel' about a near-perfect man. I had to read it in graduate school, and still can't believe Samuel Richardson sold any copies.

"Meador, put your signs in the office only—no more in the reading room. Mavis, take down another one and you'll spend the rest of your life dusting shelves."

Things quieted down a bit then. When the three of them would be in the office together, Meador would read one of his quotes aloud, positively glowing as he did so. Then Mavis devised a new tactic, answering in kind. When he offered the following:

> As good almost kill a man as kill a good book;
> who kills a man kills a reasonable creature, God's
> image; but he who destroys a good book, kills
> reason itself, kills the image of God, as it were,
> in the eye.
> —John Milton, *Areopagitica*

she retaliated with:

*Books are fatal: they are the curse of the human
race. Nine-tenths of existing books are nonsense,
and the clever books are the refutation of that
nonsense. The greatest misfortune that ever befell
man was the invention of printing.*
—Benjamin Disraeli, *Lothair XXIV*

Juanita didn't much appreciate Mavis's thus biting the hand that fed her, however poorly. But she chose not to intervene unless bloodshed seemed imminent. Meador then offered:

*Books give not wisdome where none was before,
But where some is, there reading makes it more.*
—Sir John Harington, *Epigrams I*

He had underscored the top line in red, an unsubtle hint that Mavis was refusing to learn from his brilliant selections. She countered with:

*I hate books, for they only teach people to talk
about what they do not understand.*
—Jean Jacques Rousseau: *Emile I*

About that time Juanita muttered to herself, "Why don't library-science courses teach you really useful information, like how to referee a duel between staff members?" She had even considered making volumes of quotations off-limits to both assistants, but even in a good cause wasn't ready to side with book-banners.

Eying the two newest quotations, she came to a decision. As she was being drawn into the fray anyway, she might as well participate. Settling at her desk with books of quotes and coffee from a pot on the worktable, she considered and rejected responses, finally settling for a mild one:

> *Friends will be much apart. They will respect*
> *more each other's privacy than their communion.*
> —Thoreau, *Journal*, February 22, 1841

She doubted Mavis would appreciate it, but Meador would like the fact both he and Juanita had quoted their recent Books subject.

After posting her choice, Juanita went to the reading room, where Mavis sat alone at the circulation desk. She met Juanita's gaze unsmilingly, mouth set in a line, and continued re-inking a stamp pad.

"Anything going on?" Juanita climbed onto a stool beside Mavis.

"No."

"Did a Miss Prescott phone? She's an elementary teacher who wants to arrange a time to bring her class."

"Nobody called." Mavis's tone wasn't exactly frosty, but wouldn't have quick-thawed a steak.

To be rid of her for a while, Juanita sent her to the periodicals stacks in the basement to prepare magazines for the bindery. After Mavis left, Juanita sat quietly contemplating her surroundings.

Rays of afternoon sunlight angled through tall windows at the room's far end, bathing it in a lustrous haze. Books lined three walls and several low alcoves surrounding tables and chairs, in one of which two community college students sat with heads together over a textbook. The fourth wall held forward-slanting shelves displaying magazines, beside which stood an elderly man leafing through a *Field and Stream*. Wings led off in two directions to stacks and reference room. Thus surrounded by reading matter, Juanita felt as warmly content as a miser in his vault.

Her thoughts wandered to Eddie. What hold did Cooper have over him? If the boy was hanging around with such men, English grades might be the least of his worries.

She had discussed his school project with the Nguyens on returning from Wayne's last night. Bach, grateful for Juanita's assistance following the death of Bach's sister Cam, the Nguyens' original sponsor in the United States, had urged Lee to help Eddie. Lee had agreed to meet him some afternoon after school. Juanita planned to see him tonight after work to schedule the interview. Maybe he would even open up to her about Cooper, she thought optimistically.

Right. And maybe computers were a passing fad.

Last night Bach had also told Juanita the Bromptons' ski mask was definitely yellow and green, to her considerable relief. Not only were both Bromptons good friends of hers now, but she and Cyril had a history, their families neighbors for years. She had been a bookish kid who adored him, he a shy teenager who received her adulation with amused acceptance. Shared insecurities and a genuine liking for each other had made them unlikely pals.

Her reverie ended as Meador returned from shelving books and went to the office. He quickly came out, round face flushed, sat next to Juanita and gave her a sidelong glance. "Smart aleck."

"You should've seen the rejects."

He fiddled with a ballpoint. "Like what?"

She showed him an entry she had copied:

I well believe
Thou wilt not utter what thou dost not know,
And so far will I trust thee.
—Shakespeare, *I Henry IV II. iii.*

He fought a smile. "Not bad."

She moved her hand to show him another. "This one

tempted me even more."

> *Three may keep a secret if two of them are dead.*
> —Benjamin Franklin, *Poor Richard's Almanack*

He chuckled, standoffishness evaporating. When Mavis returned from the basement, she found them chatting companionably. Throwing a questioning glance at Meador, she went into the office. He and Juanita avoided each other's eyes. Minutes went by. Juanita surmised her subordinate was trying to decide on a reply.

When Mavis did come out, she pointedly ignored them, crossing to a computer on the checkout desk and typing onto it from a handwritten list of magazines. Tension built. Finally Meador broke it.

"You like Andrew Garve, Mavis?" Eyes ingenuous, he extolled the writer's virtues as if confident of his nemesis's interest.

She turned and bestowed a dirty look on him, her mouth a petulant sliver. "Mysteries? Waste of time."

"How about P. D. James? Or Conan Doyle?"

"Doyle, shmoyle. I told you what I think of mysteries. Don't you ever listen?"

Meador and Juanita risked glancing at each other, and he emitted a snicker. This evidence of goings-on behind her back proved too much for Mavis. Hands planted on hips, gray eyes snapping with anger, she glared at Juanita.

"Some people want to keep their own little secrets, but sure do nose around in other people's business." She turned to her former collaborator, now leaning coolly on the counter. "And some jump from one side to the other like a frog in hot ashes." She stalked off, her skinny form stiff with vexation.

Meador grinned at Juanita, twirled his pen and actually began to hum under his breath.

So he had for once refused to take Mavis seriously, finally realizing what a powerful weapon good-natured tolerance could be. The down side, Juanita thought, was that Mavis would be in a worse mood than usual.

But with her, that would be a fairly subtle difference.

Chapter Thirteen

That afternoon Roy Boston approached the library counter, puffing from the exertion of climbing the outside steps. He wiped perspiration from his chubby face and laid three returns on the counter in front of Meador, who was studying figures on the computer screen.

"Good afternoon," Boston said jovially.

Meador and Juanita echoed the greeting.

"Nice out there," the attorney went on. "Warmer than the past couple of days."

Juanita agreed, got his requested books from under the counter, accepted his library card and checked them out. He turned to go, then snapped his fingers and fumbled in a jacket pocket.

"May as well give you my Friends of the Library dues. I keep forgetting to mail a check." He took out a pen and a checkbook and began to write.

Meador had turned from the monitor to Boston's returned books and was about to check one in when Juanita waved him away.

"I'll take care of that, Meador. You go see if Mavis needs help. Those magazines are heavy."

Boston paused, a flicker of surprise in his eyes. Meador obediently left. The attorney resumed writing.

"You know, Roy," Juanita mused, "I was going through some old newspapers and came across an article about the rezoning for the shopping center."

"Yes?"

"Quite a battle at City Council that night."

"All parties felt strongly about the matter. That's often the way with zoning cases."

"Some pretty nasty things got said."

"Indeed. I presume this is headed somewhere, Miss Wills?" Boston tore out the check and handed it over.

"Thanks. It occurred to me that old case could explain the attack on Rev. Asher. He seems to be a man without enemies, but maybe he made some that evening."

He did his trademark chin rub. "Possible, I suppose."

"Maybe someone is holding a grudge over his opposition?"

"I really doubt it." Boston's eyebrows raised. "You don't mean me? Well, I'll be—you do." He smiled, tucked his shirt over his substantial middle and hitched up his pants. "I assure you, Miss Wills, I haven't time to nurse grievances. Anyway, arguments in court or at public meetings are a kind of game. Tempers cool."

"Maybe for lawyers. But for someone else—"

"If you're thinking of Mr. Leggatt, my client in the shopping-center matter, he's the least vengeful person I know."

"Speaking of grudges, you and Earl Trevethan sure seemed edgy toward each other in Books the other evening."

"I'm sure Trevethan ticks everyone off sooner or later, though I believe Darrow's still his favorite opponent." The attorney smiled again. "Do all these questions mean our favorite amateur detective is working on the Asher case? I wish you luck, Miss Wills, but you're way off base suspecting me.

"If you should get into checking alibis for Monday evening, however, mine's rock-solid—I was at City Council meeting. Ask Trevethan or Pugh." He strode out.

Juanita watched the heavy door close behind him. She already had a witness to his presence at that meeting, Vivian. Anyway, he was probably a bit heavy for Paunchy Guy.

She was stamping the call slip in a battered copy of *The Shining*, returned by Boston, when a slip of paper fell out. It had a string of letters and numbers printed on it:

```
DV'IV    LM   GSV   NLEV   ZG   OZHG!
HKVXRZO  FMRG GL  NVVG ZG  GSV  UZIN
GFVHWZB  ZG  10:00  K.N.
                    GSV   NZQLI
```

Over the years, forgotten bookmarks Juanita had found in library books had included cancelled checks, dollar bills, personal letters and even credit cards. Returning the items usually brought surprised laughs from owners. Once when she had returned a notice from the Internal Revenue Service, the recipient had turned scarlet.

Boston must have grabbed up one of his kids' "secret messages" to mark his place, Juanita thought with a chuckle, recalling her own days of playing "spy" with friends. Their codes had been painfully easy to break—substituting "1" for "A" and "2" for "B," or at their most enigmatic "1" for "Z" and "26" for "A"—although they had been convinced no one else could decipher them. In her teens she had devoured newspaper cryptograms, and as an adult had often watched "Wheel of Fortune" during solitary suppers.

This particular note had intriguing aspects. "10:00 K.N." could mean "ten o'clock a.m." or "p.m." The apostrophe in the first word probably signaled a contraction. Most interesting of all, the first line contained an exclamation point.

Having nothing pressing at the moment, Juanita copied the message onto another sheet of paper, sharpened a pencil and printed "a.m." above "K.N." Then she noticed only one other "K" appeared in the puzzle, suggesting that it stood for a letter less common than a vowel. She changed "a" to "p" and wrote "p's" and "m's" above the other "K" and the "N's."

The door opened, admitting three lively youngsters and signaling that quiet time was over. Juanita stowed the cipher in a drawer and forgot it.

After work she drove to Wagoner's service station and

entered the office, where Eddie was ringing up a sale to Doug Darrow. All three said hello.

"So Machiavelli's next for Books," Doug said to Juanita as he handed Eddie a credit card. "You read *The Prince* yet?"

"Years ago. I need to review it. You?"

"Nya-a-ah, but I can wing it. Everybody knows ol' Mac said 'the end justifies the means.'"

"That isn't quite all."

"Just kidding, teach—I'll read it. At least it's shorter than *Middlemarch*."

Juanita asked Eddie if he could meet Lee Nguyen on Tuesday afternoon at the library, where she could be handy to help in case the two had communication problems.

"Then you'll write the paper, and I'll look it over and make suggestions."

The teenager agreed without enthusiasm.

"Getting tutoring in English, Eddie?" Doug asked.

Eddie, frowning at a credit card form he was filling out, shrugged affirmatively.

"You know, you could be doing better in history too."

"Cain't remember all those dates and names."

"There's lots more to history than those." Doug signed the form. "Tell you what, why don't I give you extra help? What's your free period at school?"

They discovered that the times Eddie was free Doug was in class, and vice versa. But Doug persisted, lean face kind but determined.

"Drop by my farm some evening, then. I'll teach you a few techniques for remembering the material."

The teen shook his head. "I work here nights till nine, 'cept Mondays and Thursdays I get off when Dad gets back from supper." Face flushing, he quickly added, "I'm always busy Mondays, though."

"How about Thursday, next week? Around seven?"

Eddie reluctantly agreed. He handed back Doug's credit card, along with the customer copy of the form.

Juanita beamed. Doug had a reputation for mouthing off to school administrators, but also one—apparently justified—for going out of his way to encourage students.

"Thursday then. 'Bye, guys." Doug turned to go.

Juanita stopped him. "By the way, Doug, your little joke's been really cute, but the second time you phoned you got me out of a luxurious bath. So stop calling me and move on with your life, okay?"

"Juanita, love, what the Hell you talking about?"

"I'm sure you can't imagine."

"I can't."

If it wasn't the truth, he had a future as an actor.

"You haven't been phoning and hanging up without identifying yourself?"

Doug chuckled. "Sounds like you've got a secret admirer. Does he inquire what you're wearing?"

"Not exactly. You serious, you haven't called?"

"I swear it on my old mama's washboard. Of course I can understand your hoping it was me. You want me bad."

"When an armadillo wins the Kentucky Derby, Darrow."

"Seriously, Juanita, maybe you ought to change your telephone number."

"I don't want to. Mine's easy to remember and I'm used to it. Anyway, why should I be inconvenienced by some turkey who gets his jollies bugging people?"

After Doug left, Juanita visited with Eddie a few minutes, hoping he would voluntarily mention Gib Cooper. But he answered her attempts at conversation with monosyllables, eyes wary, slim face tightly controlled. Finally she raised the subject herself.

"You thought any more about what we discussed last night, Eddie?"

He stared stonily at the counter, avoiding her eyes. She pitied his discomfort, but longed to shake sense into him. At last she gave up and told him goodbye. Belatedly, he mumbled thanks for arranging the interview with Lee. As Juanita started her Chevy, she hoped he'd get more out of young Miss Nguyen than she had just now out of him.

She was at home, eating a quick supper before going out again, when the phone rang. Swallowing a bite of sandwich, she said hello. No response. She tried again, louder. Still silence. She was about to hang up when a low muffled voice spoke.

"Keep your nose out of other people's business, lady. Or else." *Click.*

Juanita held the cool receiver against her chin. If it wasn't Doug making these calls, then who? Maybe they were serious threats.

At that thought, fear fluttered inside her. Had she, without realizing it, found an important clue in the Asher case? Or was she close to turning up one? The idea of someone watching her, knowing details of her daily life, made her shudder.

Sheer melodrama, she scolded herself. The caller must be one of the Books jokers. She considered phoning Cyril Brompton, Willard Pugh and others to anonymously threaten their lives if they didn't stop bothering her. But if they recognized her voice, they would enjoy it too much. Doug and the others might compare notes, and she would really be the butt of their jokes.

Juanita finished eating, changed to slacks and looked up two addresses. If the mysterious messages were meant to frighten her off, she reflected, they would fail. In fact, she planned to do some investigating tonight.

Dusk was yielding to darkness as she eased under the Chevy's steering wheel. Her mind on questions she planned to ask, she set her purse in the passenger seat. A glance in the rearview mirror showed a lipstick smudge on her cheek, and she reached for her bag to get a tissue.

A small pointed head with beady dark eyes poked around one leather corner.

A snake!

Yanking her hand back, Juanita flung herself out the still-open car door. She fell on the drive, left arm curled beneath her body. Concrete scraped her palm.

Instinct and adrenaline brought her to her feet. She slammed the door hard and leaned shakily against it, breath coming in jerks. Juanita closed her eyes and forced herself to calm down. She was okay, really okay.

As her breathing eased and the trembling in her legs slowed, the arm she had fallen on began to hurt. She also realized a laceration on her hand was burning.

Juanita peered into the auto's interior. The dome light had gone out, but the porchlight she had left burning illumined a stout brown-and-tan-patterned body slithering over her purse. She thought it was a bullsnake, similar to one a male cousin had put in her bureau drawer when she was twelve. How he had chortled at her fright over a non-poisonous reptile!

But she wasn't sure this particular snake was harmless.

She went back to the house and checked her injuries, relieved to find they weren't severe. The arm seemed unbroken, the scraped skin not deeply cut. As she cleaned the hand, she wondered how the creature had gotten into her vehicle. It was early in the year for snakes, though the on-off unseasonably warm weather might have brought them out. She hadn't left the window open, so the unwelcome visitor hadn't simply crawled inside.

Someone had put it there.

Chapter Fourteen

While treating the wound, Juanita plotted her strategy, then got a shovel and a sturdy cardboard box from the garage and approached her vehicle. The uninvited guest now lay curled complacently on the passenger-side floorboard. Juanita set the box on the paving, spread the container's lid and gingerly opened the car door.

The reptile lifted its head and hissed. Juanita backed away.

Heart beating fast, she inched forward. The snake eyed her unblinkingly, but didn't move. Hastily Juanita shoved her scoop under it and lifted it out. It writhed, unfolding its coils. For an awful moment, she thought it would wriggle off onto the driveway.

But she got the shovel over the box just as the creature fell. Hurriedly she closed the boxtop and weighted it with a rock.

There. On her return, she would look up a picture of the reptile in her *Encyclopedia of Wildlife*. If it was a bullsnake, some farmer might welcome it as a rat-killer, or some science teacher as a classroom exhibit and pet. Sighing with relief, Juanita crawled into the Chevy and turned the ignition. The car resisted, but started on the fifth try.

As Juanita drove to Wyndham's east side, she recalled how she had been outsmarted by Amanda Burns, Avon salesperson and Doer of Good Works. Asked by Amanda for a United Way contribution, Juanita replied she preferred giving to individual charities. Undaunted, Amanda asked which ones, and Juanita gave Wyndham Relief Agency as an example. The first thing she knew she had been volunteered to drive a weekly shift in the WRA van, collecting money and cast-offs to benefit the elderly and poor. She could have refused, denied agreeing to help, but halfway admired Amanda's cheek. So she had decided to make the best of it.

The volunteering hadn't turned out so badly. Besides assisting a worthy cause, the canvassing sometimes provided Juanita interesting tidbits about goings-on in town.

She turned onto East Birmingham, where many buildings sat vacant, a haven for transients. The depressed area's few homeowners kept to themselves and seldom ventured out at night. Juanita pulled into a lot beside a rambling former warehouse, whose cavernous space allowed room for sorting, mending and storing items donated to WRA. In need of repairs but structurally sound, the building had been rented cheaply to the charity so it wouldn't sit empty. To her surprise, a white Lincoln sat beside the charity's van tonight.

Typically when Juanita arrived for a shift the warehouse would be locked, no one else around. She would fish a door key from a gravel-filled flower pot between parking lot and porch, open the building and get the van key from an unlocked desk drawer in an unlocked office. If Wayne found her security lax, WRA's practices would probably make him stroke out.

If she ever decided to tell him.

But the system ought to be good enough, she thought, resenting how she had lately been made to feel unsafe in Wyndham. "Welcome to modern life, Juanita," she muttered as she entered.

In an office off the foyer, Estelle Pugh sat at a battered desk holding a phone receiver to an ear and toying with a gold earring. In her crisp navy-and-white suit, she looked wildly out of place in the seedy surroundings.

At Juanita's step, Estelle nodded hello but continued talking. "Disappointing in the *extreme*, Mildred. We *rely* on that grant. If it *doesn't* come through—*van* collections are holding up *fairly* well, but I *doubt* they'll make up that much." She sighed heavily. "We'll have to do a *TV* spot, I suppose. It will mean *my* running over to *Tulsa* one day, but if it's *necessary* . . . ."

Noble Estelle. Juanita had wondered why the banker's wife devoted time to a ragtag outfit like WRA, society teas being more her line, until she noticed that when a media spokesperson was called for, Estelle was always handy. A funding crisis, real or manufactured, could mean an opportunity for her to be on television.

But that wasn't *totally* fair, as Estelle herself would say. She also did the mundane work of driving the collection van one evening a week.

Estelle hung up, replaced the earring and patted her hair into place. Reaching into a drawer, she handed Juanita a key.

"I wasn't expecting to see you, Estelle." Juanita tossed the key in the air and caught it one-handed. "Isn't Monday your night?"

"I was here late today for a *board* meeting and decided to make *notes* while things were *fresh* in my *mind*." Spreading a manicured hand, Estelle inspected its bright red polish. "There's no hurry on *dinner*. Willard's working *late*."

"Does he work lots of evenings? You must get lonely." Juanita threw the key higher and deftly fielded it. Heaving it yet farther, she bagged it with the other hand.

Estelle looked blank. "*Lonely?* Oh, you mean without *Willard*. Not really. We're *both* out a lot. He *works* one or two nights a *week*, goes to lots of *meetings*—lodge, City *Council* and such." She inspected the other hand. "I have *my* clubs and *sorority*. We go to *Books* together, of course."

Juanita flung the key again and tried catching it behind her. It clattered to the floor, along with her brief juggling career.

"I understand this week's council meeting lasted till eleven or so. Did Willard have to stay the whole time?"

"Must have," Estelle said, absorbed in pushing back a cuticle. "It was around eleven-*thirty* when he got home."

So, Juanita thought as she retrieved the key. Vivian had

said Pugh left the meeting about eight-thirty. He had had three hours to meet co-conspirators, vandalize a church, beat up its minister and get home by eleven-thirty.

Piece of cake.

Of course the fact he had had time didn't mean he had actually done all that.

From a bulletin board on one wall, Juanita unhooked a photocopied town map showing her designated collection zone. Three marked addresses in other areas denoted places to pick up called-in items.

"Ta," she told Estelle, getting a vague wave in return.

Juanita climbed into the old WRA van. Given by someone for a tax deduction, it had been decorated by an apparently color-blind staff member from donated remnants of paint. Top, hood and back were barn-red, one side white, the other lime green. On both sides "Wyndham Relief Agency" glowed purple, along with yellow flowers and turquoise stars. Juanita suspected even aging flower children would find it garish.

Tonight's route lay through northwest Wyndham, a section whose residents were mostly prosperous professionals. That would seem to bode well for collections, except Juanita had learned disposable income and generosity didn't necessarily correspond.

She turned onto Main Street, keyed up at thought of the investigating ahead. As she drove through downtown, her headlights picking out the computer store's sign, she remembered Cooper and wondered if the snake was his revenge for her identifying him to Wayne.

Was he also her mysterious caller? Had the creature been placed in her car to lend credence to those warnings?

Recalling Cooper's penetrating eyes, Juanita involuntarily jerked the steering wheel. The van veered sharply to the right. Bouncing off the curb, it angled hard to the left. She fought for control, narrowly missing an oncoming pickup truck.

Shape up and drive, Juanita, she admonished herself.

She would tell Wayne tomorrow about the snake and those phone calls.

Wait, though. He would ask what the caller had said. What would she reply? A warning not to snoop implied she had been snooping. She decided she would take her chances with a possibly murderous computer repairman rather than a definitely homicidal cop.

Besides, even if Cooper was trying to shake her up, he surely wouldn't risk actually harming her. He had to know Wayne would come after him for it. If Eddie didn't recant, Cooper was probably home free on Asher's beating—unless he called attention to himself with more violence.

All the same, she planned to be careful.

Juanita turned into tree-lined Fourth Avenue, an area she hadn't canvassed before. Two-story frame homes mixed with one-story bricks, and street lights revealed late-model autos and station wagons in driveways. Carrying a bank bag holding change and a receipt pad, she walked up Fourth, stopping at houses and casually bringing up the church incident. She got many tsk-tsks and little else, but did collect some money and a sturdy chest of drawers, obligingly loaded in the van by its donor.

At a buff brick in the third block, Katherine Greer answered the bell, smiling as she recognized Juanita.

"Miss Wills. What brings you out tonight?" Katherine wiped a hand on an immaculate pink apron and beckoned Juanita inside. The living room, full of polished wood surfaces, soft green carpet and white and peach upholstery, looked exactly right for Katherine. When Juanita explained her errand, the retired teacher took a handbag from a desk.

"I can spare a few dollars. Did you enjoy the discussion Monday?"

"Interesting. I thought you might have to break up a

fight."

Katherine laughed, her blue-gray eyes huge behind strong lenses. "Thoreau always seems to provoke arguments. And you people are especially passionate for a book-study group." She opened a coin purse and removed a roll of bills.

"Before the meeting began," Juanita said carefully, "we were talking about the Asher beating. Some thought there must be a militia group operating around here."

"Is that right?" Katherine handed her a few ones.

"Thanks." Juanita counted them and began writing a receipt. "But it seems unlikely. I mean, we'd know, wouldn't we? People in Waco knew about the Branch Davidians."

"How long have you lived in Wyndham, Miss Wills?"

Juanita glanced up, struck by an odd note in the older woman's voice. The wrinkled face now looked tired.

"I grew up here, moved away after high school, came back five years ago."

The magnified eyes narrowed. "I've been here all my life except for college at Norman and a hitch in the WACs. It doesn't seem an unlikely possibility to me."

"Really? Have you heard of a militia around here?"

Katherine opened her mouth, then abruptly closed it. Her finger traced the carved desk edge. "History's full of intolerance," she said at last, "and some people can't stand for others to think differently from the way they do."

"Sure, but—a paramilitary outfit here?"

"Hate exists everywhere. And some is organized."

Juanita handed Katherine the receipt and left, thinking about their conversation. She couldn't suspect the Books moderator of involvement in whatever was going on in Wyndham, but did wonder why the usually forthright woman had retreated into generalities when asked that direct question.

Juanita strode up the walk of a Dutch colonial, where two boys and a dog played under a yard light. A tossed football came within inches of her face. She pushed the doorbell. A slender dark-haired woman answered, listened to Juanita's spiel while keeping one eye on the roughhousing.

"I guess that isn't lethal yet," she said with a grin. "Come in. I've some children's clothes you can have."

Juanita followed her into a cluttered living room where Roy Boston's bulk nearly filled a leather recliner. In his shirtsleeves and stocking feet, he sat polishing an army boot. An array of footwear sat on a newspaper in front of him. Mrs. Boston went to get the clothes.

"'Scuse my not getting up," Boston said with a wave at the collection on the paper. "Have a chair. I didn't realize you worked for WRA—don't believe I've seen you out in the van before."

"I haven't been driving it long." Juanita sat on an over-stuffed couch and tried to make conversation. "Sturdy-looking shoe you have there."

"Combat boots never seem to wear out." Boston inspected his handiwork. "Great for tramping about in the cold."

"I thought you didn't like the outdoors."

"Not true. When I have a difficult case, a walk in the fresh air clears my head."

Juanita's fingers pleated and unpleated her purse strap as she searched for something else to say. She remembered the cipher.

"I found something in a book you returned today."

The hand applying polish paused. He frowned. "Oh?"

"A slip of paper with letters and numbers on it."

Boston's brow visibly relaxed. He set the boot down and rubbed his chin. "Letters and numbers? Doesn't mean any-thing to me."

Juanita waved a hand in dismissal. "Probably something of your children's you picked up to use as a bookmark."

"Could be."

Mrs. Boston returned with an armful of small garments. "I've washed these, but some need mending—torn pockets and such."

Juanita saw at a glance the clothing was good quality. She told the Bostons thanks and goodbye. Following a stretch where few residents were home, she reached the end of her assigned part of Fourth Avenue, crossed the street and started down the other side.

At a picket-fenced white house that fairly shouted "small-town America," a woman in housedress and loafers opened the door. Wispy graying hair and a fatigued air made her look sixty, though she might be only fifty. She invited Juanita in, asked her to wait and went to another room, where she could be heard opening and closing drawers.

The living room had a wildlife motif, with prints of pheasants on walls and a stuffed owl and painted duck decoys atop a bookcase. Juanita gravitated to a shelf of hardback tomes about various wars, biographies of generals and battle analyses. Then she spotted a cache of paperbacks with ominous titles that included *Armageddon in America*, *The White Race in Retreat* and *Defending America with Rifles and Handguns*.

Juanita picked up one and leafed through it. The paper was rough, the print amateurish, the message unmistakable:

The U.S.A. was threatened from without and within, and true patriots must be prepared to take up arms. The phrase "guardians of liberty" recurred often. As she was returning the volume to its slot, the woman came back. Juanita smiled apologetically.

"I hope you don't mind. I'm a librarian, and can't resist looking at books wherever I go."

"Those are Walt's—I'm not much of a reader myself." She handed Juanita a dollar bill and some change.

"Thanks. How should I make out the receipt?"

"To Jenny Fuller."

Something clicked in Juanita's mind. "Is your husband by any chance the Walt Fuller who runs the water department?"

"Yes. You know my husband?"

"Not well. I've seen him at council meetings. And I believe that was him I saw talking to Mariette Asher at the hospital the other day."

"Asher? Isn't that the name of the preacher who got beat up on?"

"Yes, I guess your husband must know him."

Jenny nodded dismissively, as if Walt knew lots of people she didn't.

Juanita could barely contain her excitement long enough to write the receipt and bid Jenny goodbye. Walt Fuller was portly, like Paunchy Guy. And at the hospital he had asked Mariette whether Asher had waked up "at all." Maybe he was afraid the minister would identify him as one of the attackers? After seeing Fuller's preferred reading, Juanita thought that a real possibility.

Three blocks along, she came to the Bromptons' Cape Cod. Rosy-cheeked Eva, in sprightly aqua culottes, let her in. "We're about to have dessert, Juanita. You'll join us, won't you?"

Juanita agreed. They went through the living and dining rooms to a cozy blue-and-white-chintz breakfast nook. Cyril sat at the table, the lit chandelier reflected in his bald head. Eva served coffee she had ground and blended herself, and Juanita declined cream and sugar. Cyril cut a piece of dense apricot pound cake for her.

"Recovered from your excitement?" he said. At Juanita's puzzled look, he added, "You know, Monday, when you found Rev. Asher."

"Oh yes, that seems a long time ago." She ate a bite of cake, savored the delicate fruit flavor. "How's your elderly neighbor doing? Mr. Lange?"

Cyril dropped the cake he was placing on his wife's plate. With an affectionate smile at him, Eva rescued it. "We don't have a neighbor named Lange," she said. "You have us confused with someone else."

Her husband's precision in severing the next slice would have done credit to a gem-cutter tackling the Hope Diamond.

"My mistake," Juanita said hurriedly. "This coffee's terrific. The cake too."

Eva shrugged self-deprecatingly. They chatted about the weather, agreeing that winter seemed about over.

"Speaking of winter," Juanita said, "I think next year I'll try skiing. I gather people from here go mostly to New Mexico or Colorado. You ever ski, Cyril?"

"Sometimes, principally at Angel Fire. I'm surprised to hear you're taking it up."

"Why? You think I'm not athletic enough?"

"No-o-o, people of all sizes, ages and abilities ski. But what put the idea in your head?"

Juanita sipped her coffee, inhaling the heady aroma. "I saw a documentary recently, and it looked like fun. You ski, Eva?"

"A little. I'm better at apres-ski."

"You own a fancy snowsuit, goggles, ski mask, all that?"

For an instant Cyril looked startled. Or perhaps the light was glinting in his green eyes.

"Of course." Eva gave her a curious look.

When Juanita had finished eating and collected a few dollars, she left and worked her way back to the van. She got in and turned onto Birch Street, thinking about the last interview. Both Bromptons skied, so they probably owned another mask besides the one Bach had seen, maybe one in purple and yellow. Cyril wasn't built like any of the vandals, but could have lent a mask to someone else. Being mixed up in anything violent, however, seemed out of character for the easygoing abstracter.

Juanita didn't want him involved, for his own sake and Eva's.

But she did feel sure of one thing: Something was fishy about that package he had collected for "Mr. Lange."

Chapter Fifteen

Juanita finished her assigned route and the call-ins and decided she had time for two unscheduled stops whose addresses she had copied before leaving home. She pulled up at a red-brick ranch where clumps of winter-hardy weeds passed for a lawn. Clouds shrouded the moon. The evening had become chilly, and she snuggled into a sweater she had brought.

She rang the bell and waited. Soon Earl Trevethan appeared, wearing faded jeans and work shirt. When she explained she was collecting for Wyndham Relief Agency, his eyes narrowed.

"Someone was by a few nights ago. I thought you folks didn't canvass the same area week after week."

Juanita apologized, saying she must have gotten confused about her assigned boundaries.

"Okay, no problem." He started to shut the door.

"Since I'm here anyway," she said quickly, "could I see some of your woodwork? Willard Pugh says it's beautiful."

Trevethan's demeanor changed. Grinning, he threw the door wide. "Certainly—always glad to show it off."

She followed him through neat but Spartan living and dining rooms and an antiseptic kitchen, into a back yard of dead weeds bisected by a path to a white frame building. Trevethan's housewifery apparently quit at his home's outer door.

"See these thick walls," he said, ushering her into the small structure. "They keep the neighbors from yelling about noise."

Just inside the shop door, a battered desk held hot plate, coffeepot and dishes. A cot sat on one wall. Juanita guessed this workshop was Trevethan's real home. It also housed an array of equipment, radial saw to lathe, and wood projects in various stages of finishing. With justifiable pride, he showed her a partly assembled chair, a bookcase headboard between coats of varnish and a completed table with an inlaid top of variously colored and grained wood pieces in a geometric pattern.

"Beautiful," Juanita murmured, touching the table top.

He slid a hand along one side, touched a hidden spring. A tiny drawer shot from what had seemed a solid panel.

"Oh!" she gasped in surprise.

Trevethan chuckled, clearly enjoying himself.

This was a side of him she had never seen before, she thought. But just then she glimpsed a collection of objects that reminded her of her real errand. A rifle and a shotgun stood against one wall. On nails above them hung an olive-drab jacket, fatigues and camouflage gear. For a second she felt vulnerable, alone with Trevethan and his weapons in a building that would muffle any outcry.

But his tender caress of the secret drawer reassured her. She shook off the thought.

"You know, Earl, when anything's happening in Wyndham, whether it's a music program, flea market or whatever, you're always there."

"Yeah. So?"

"You have this great talent, and it must occupy lots of time. Why do you go to City Council meetings, for instance?"

He slid the drawer into its hiding place. "Why not? They're live drama. And aren't we supposed to get involved, know what's going on in our government?"

"Most people don't take that so literally."

"I do." He straightened to his full height, several inches taller than she. "Are you implying something?"

She cleared her throat nervously. "I was looking at an old newspaper that had a big article about the fight over the new shopping center. I noticed you spoke for the rezoning."

"Again, so?"

"If you didn't own land nearby, why'd you feel so strongly about it?"

"I was standing up for a principle, like your pet Thoreau *claimed* he did. People shouldn't try to tell others what they can do with their own property."

"Even if added traffic in that area should cause some little kid to get killed?"

Trevethan's tone turned frosty. "Another bleeding-heart liberal. Just like Ferris Asher."

"Did you two hold a grudge after that fight?"

"How the hell would I know how Asher felt?"

The comradely atmosphere in the workshop had vanished. "What about you? Did you stay mad about it?"

"So that's what this is about. You think I had something to do with Asher's beating."

Her silence gave assent.

"That's why you really came tonight. You knew I'd already been canvassed." He crossed the shop in two strides, flung the door open and waved her out with a sweeping mock-gallant gesture. "Out. Now."

The order was melodramatic but effective. She sauntered across the room, deliberately not hurrying, trying to look taller than her stocky 5'5". As she glanced at the desk this time, she noticed a stack of papers beside the coffeepot, the top sheet of which looked familiar. It wasn't till Trevethan had escorted her through his house and out the front door that she realized it was one of the slanderous campaign posters.

She paused getting into the van. Had he brought one home as a curiosity? Or had he been distributing them?

As Juanita drove to her second planned stop, she passed the large Tudor of stucco, half-timbering and gray stone where she knew Willard and Estelle Pugh lived. Impulsively, she stopped.

A housekeeper in housedress and striped apron showed her to a den furnished with finely crafted early-American furniture, then departed. Estelle Pugh, hair perfectly coiffed but now attired in sweater and slacks, lay on a couch watching a sitcom. As Juanita entered, Estelle rose and switched off the TV.

"Sit *down*, please. Like something to drink?"

Juanita sat. "No, thanks. I must get home. You seemed worried earlier about WRA finances, so I thought you'd like to know tonight's collections were good. A few pieces of furniture, lots of clothing and a couple hundred dollars."

"Good, *good*. Glad to *hear* it." Estelle neither smiled nor sounded particularly enthusiastic. Had she been looking forward to that TV appearance?

Willard Pugh strolled in, elf-like in a red cashmere jumpsuit. He tossed a pamphlet on the coffee table near Juanita.

"Thought I heard voices. How are you, Miss Wills?"

"She was just telling me the *donations* were *good* tonight, Willard. Who *were* some people you *collected* from?"

Juanita mentioned several. "Mrs. Boston gave a stack of very nice children's clothes, some almost new."

"Oh *yes*," Estelle nodded, patting her helmet of hair. "Those kids get the *best*, and *never* wear clothes out because they have so *many*. How about the *Rodgerses* and the *Bechtels*? *They* were on your *route*, and they're usually *very* generous."

As Juanita enumerated other contributors, she realized one reason Estelle worked for WRA was the chance to learn what others gave away. Juanita could identify, though her own curiosity concerned people's behavior more than their possessions.

Pugh listened politely, his expression amused. At a lull in the conversation, he mentioned the race for county commissioner. "I hope I can count on your vote for Shipman."

"I haven't decided yet. Neither he nor Piersall strikes me as someone who ought to be running the county."

He chuckled. "I wouldn't want Jesse in charge of the nation's space program, but I think he can handle building roads and administering county funds. He's at least honest."

"You don't think Piersall is?"

Pugh tented his fingertips. "Let's say he was strangely determined to approve rezoning for that new shopping center."

"You saying you think he was bribed?"

"The opposition's arguments clearly bored him."

Juanita mentioned the savage anti-Piersall placards she had seen. Pugh's reaction surprised her.

"Vulgar tripe! Garbage like that hasn't any place in a campaign."

"I agree. But it wasn't directed against your man, Mr. Shipman. It could even help him."

Pugh eyed Juanita as if she were a slow-witted three-year-old. "That's precisely the problem, Miss Wills. Shipman is Piersall's only real competition, so everybody assumes we put out that poster. Doesn't do any good to deny it. The sympathy vote could help Piersall win."

"Don't talk *politics*, Willard. It's *boring*," said Estelle. Her tone switched from scolding to insinuating. "I heard something *interesting* about a fellow *Books* member today. Doug Darrow."

Her listeners waited expectantly.

"He's having *orgies* at that *farm* where he lives."

Pugh found his tongue first. "Orgies—Estelle, you can't be serious."

"I heard it today at the *beauty* shop." Estelle's eyes had grown animated, her horsey face pink with excitement. "He gets *high* school *boys* out there at *night*, and *awful* things go on. *Drugs*, *sex*, God *knows* what."

"Now, Estelle, that's just beauty-parlor chitchat. How would anyone know what happens out there anyway?"

"*I* heard the information, not *you*, Willard. And I'd believe it over your lodge cronies' tales any day." She said young men had been seen going into the farmhouse several at a time. "Last *Monday* night somebody saw at *least* ten or twelve boys. And they stayed *quite* a while, from what I hear."

"Someone actually hid and watched till they left?" Pugh scoffed.

Estelle," Juanita said, "I bet one of Doug's classes was having a party. Or else he was tutoring some students."

Pugh seconded her, adding that the rumor seemed on a par with the tasteless campaign poster. His wife remained unconvinced. Juanita ostentatiously checked her watch, saying she had to be going. As she got up to leave, she glanced at the pamphlet on the coffee table.

"What are you reading, Willard? *The Patriot Besieged.* What's that about?"

He looked sheepish. "Earl insisted on lending it to me the other evening. Rather a radical publication—all about the threat to America posed by dissenters."

Juanita opened the thin book and skimmed a few lines. "So we need to repeal the Bill of Rights, eh? Can't say I'm in favor of savaging the Constitution."

"Nor I."

Juanita drove away, disturbed to realize material like that pamphlet and Fuller's books was finding an audience in Wyndham. Could such reading matter be a recruiting device for a hate group? It was a scary thought.

Estelle's accusation about Doug also rankled. Though Juanita liked a good rumor herself, this seemed a particularly vicious one. Surely some innocent activity had been misinterpreted. But loose talk about it could jeopardize Doug's job.

On the other hand, his offer to tutor Eddie now bothered her. That was the insidious thing about gossip. You could protest you didn't believe it, but it affected your thinking about people involved anyway.

Chapter Sixteen

The other address Juanita had copied proved to be the north end of a green duplex in an undistinguished part of south Wyndham. Paint was peeling, and the occupants apparently shared Trevethan's view of gardening: the less the better. She drove past twice, curious but with no intention of stopping.

Gib Cooper lived here.

She was passing the dwelling a third time when the resident himself, wearing jeans and pullover, stepped out the door. At sight of his burr haircut and rippling muscles, Juanita swallowed hard. But by the time he closed the door and turned around, she had passed him and gone beyond the nearest street light. Idling along, she watched in her rearview mirror while he got into a recent-model beige coupe and drove away.

That changed her plans. She parked a block from the duplex and started canvassing again, striking up conversations and mentioning she had a friend named Cooper living somewhere in the area.

"Seems like it might be that green duplex in the next block," she would say, "but I'm not sure. Do you know the people who live there?"

No one did, till she reached the duplex's other side. A skinny gentleman of about seventy-five, wearing baggy sweater and slacks, answered her knock. At mention of WRA, he smiled and invited Juanita into a living room littered with clothing, newspapers and dirty dishes. The place had the musty, medicinal odor she thought of as "old people's smell," the reason she had hated visiting a great-grandmother when she was a child.

A rounder old man, dressed in coveralls and seated in a grungy platform rocker, glanced up from a TV on the coffee table. His slender housemate shouted her errand in his ear. While Juanita pretended not to hear, the two men loudly discussed whether to donate anything. The first man won, asked her to wait a minute and went to another room. The second again focused on his TV program.

Juanita waited guiltily, wishing she could leave without a donation since the two appeared a short step from needing WRA's help themselves. When the thin man returned, he proudly handed her $1.67 in coin. She thanked him, wrote a receipt to the names given her and asked about her "friend" Cooper. The first man nodded eagerly.

"He lives right next to us, has for near a year. Keeps to himself, don't throw wild parties. Good neighbor. You oughta stop in and visit him. Don't think he's there now, though. I saw him go out a little bit ago."

"Hush, Ben," said the other. "You talk too much. Mr. Cooper wouldn't want you discussing him with a door-to-door solicitor."

Thus put in her place, Juanita soon said goodbye. Her questions at homes on the other side of the duplex brought no further information.

She was about to climb back into the van when she had another idea. On Cooper's end of the duplex she had noticed a window with the shade partly up. She shut the van door, strolled casually to the window and looked in. The shade stopped four inches above the sill, giving a good view of Cooper's living room, especially since he had helpfully left a lamp on.

Vivian had not exaggerated. Weapons lay everywhere: pistols, a rifle or two, a machine gun, machetes and knives. Juanita wondered if he had the proper permits.

A large map of Vietnam dotted with pins hung on a side wall, while on another were magazine photos, some peaceful scenes of village life, others mute records of wartime destruction. On the wall facing her, a knife handle protruded from a close-up of a man's head. Gashes in the picture spoke of habitual target practice.

Cooper did seem obsessed. But did that make him dangerous? Or was this shrine to the war helping him work out inner turmoil?

It was growing late. Deciding she had seen all she could tonight, Juanita returned to the van and drove off.

She reached WRA headquarters, where her own car now sat alone, and parked the van next to the office, leaving the clothing and furniture locked inside for agency volunteers to unload tomorrow. She left the van key in the office and the one to the building in the flower pot, then tried to start the Chevy. It made the "r-r-r-r" noise she had become all too familiar with, but this time started after four tries. She drove through town, stopping by Federal National Bank to drop a bank bag of donated money into the night depository.

At home she put the car in the garage and went to look in the box she had left standing by the porch, planning to refresh her memory on the snake's markings before looking it up. But the rock now lay beside the carton, the lid open. The reptile had vanished.

Chapter Seventeen

Friday morning proved gloomy, both outside and in. Juanita woke to a steady drizzle falling from a mousey sky. The Chevy adamantly refused to start, so she walked to work with wind whipping chilly rain against her legs. At the library Mavis still wasn't talking, and Meador's expression reflected the somber weather. Juanita shut herself in the office to catch up on correspondence, coffee at her elbow, radio tuned to an "easy listening" station.

But as she typed, her mind wandered to events of the previous evening. When she proofread a printed-out letter with "volume" spelled "volum" and "column" as "colume," she exited the software and gave herself up to brooding.

Although she had learned Trevethan had a soft, creative side, overall he impressed her as a bully, perhaps the type to be involved in intimidation and violence. He had not been one of Asher's attackers, since she felt certain Cooper was Athletic Guy, but maybe he had helped harass the Nguyens? He often disparaged minorities, and his gray sedan might have been the light-colored car from which the garbage was thrown. The passenger on the side closest her house had looked too thin for him, but Trevethan could have been the driver.

Recalling the placard in his workshop, Juanita phoned Sharpe Printers and spoke to owner Burt Sharpe.

"Hi, Burt, it's Juanita Wills. I know you sometimes print campaign posters, and I'm wondering if you did one lately that's anti-Piersall. A really nasty one."

He laughed. "I know the one you mean, but I don't accept such garbage. Besides, the one I saw was shoddy, off-register. Never catch me turning out work like that."

"Thanks, Burt. I didn't think you'd done it." She called other printers, with the same results. She doubted the handbill had been computer-generated—at least she had never seen a software program with such pictures. Dejected at reaching a dead end, she drummed her fingers on the phone book.

Piersall. That name reminded her of Willard Pugh's bribery allegation against the councilman. If the council members' opinions about the shopping-center zoning had been evenly divided, buying only one vote could have assured its passage. And from seeing the body in action, Juanita knew Piersall also exerted influence over two of the other four members.

An intriguing possibility, but she couldn't think how to check it out.

Then there was the matter of Pugh's own whereabouts last Monday. According to Vivian, he hadn't been at the meeting all evening. Size-wise, Pugh could have been Teeny Guy. But Juanita kept coming up against the question of T.G.'s vacillating behavior, totally unlike the banker's usual self-assured manner.

She twisted her torso to ease a kink in her back, then went to the window and raised the blinds, looking out at a dun-colored world. The rain had picked up, driving hard against the glass. "Sounds of Silence" concluded on the radio, then a voice announced a thunderstorm watch for northeastern Oklahoma for the next three hours. Juanita returned to her chair.

The pamphlet at the Pughs' home and the right-wing books at the Fullers' bothered her. As a consumer of everything from bodice-rippers to Jane Austen novels to cereal-box patter if no book or magazine was handy, she wasn't one to condemn people for their reading. But if a Klan-type group had targeted Asher, possession of such materials might give a clue to its membership. Add to that Fuller's curiosity about whether the minister had regained consciousness, and you had. . . .

Zilch. Anyway, if Fuller were a member of this alleged secret organization, would he leave its propaganda in his living room for a casual visitor to see?

Juanita's thoughts strayed to Cyril Brompton and the elusive Mr. Lange. All at once, an idea occurred to her. The scurrilous campaign posters might have been printed out of town and mailed to someone in Wyndham, in a package the same size and shape as Cyril's. She had also seen the abstracter later that same day, entering the building where Roy Boston had his office, carrying a similar packet. Maybe Cyril, Boston and Trevethan were all involved in trashing Piersall.

Her brain reeling with possibilities, Juanita remembered the cipher from *The Shining* and decided it might clear her head to work on it. She went to the reading room and took it from the checkout counter drawer, Mavis watching her in frigid silence.

Back in the office, Juanita noticed that the combination "GSV" appeared three times in the message, including once in the signature. She tried common three-letter words, eliminating "for" because that would make "GL" translate as "f_." Implausible. "Not" wouldn't work because then "GL" would be "n_," which couldn't be "no" since "L" and "S" wouldn't both stand for "o." She tried "and." "GL" could then be "as," but "ZG" would be "_a." "Fa," "ma" or "pa"? Not likely.

That left "the." She wrote it above "GSV" and filled in

```
  e  e          the    m  e     t         t
DV' IV    LM    GSV    NLEV    ZG     OZHG!


  pe           t    t    meet    t      the
HKVXRZO      FMRG   GL    NVVG   ZG     GSV


   m    t e          t    10:00   p.m.
UZIN,   GFVHWZB     ZG    10:00   K.N.


                  the  m
                  GSV NZQLI
```

letters correspondingly throughout the puzzle. She now had:

The middle part seemed to say "to meet at the," followed by "at 10:00 p.m." Tingling with the joy of the chase, Juanita put "o" above "L" and "a" above "Z" throughout the cipher.

Something about the puzzle now struck her. "Z" represented "a" and "N" stood for "M." Could the code be a simple reversal of the alphabet?

She was about to test that theory when a phone call sent her to the reference room to look up information. There, two elderly females asked for guidance in tracking down genealogical material. She assisted the caller, then the women, having to repeat directions for the latter several times.

Juanita was crossing the main reading room heading back to her office when the door opened and Wayne walked in. His face was stony, his mouth a thin line. He nodded to Mavis and formally asked Juanita if he could speak with her.

When they were closeted in the office, she spread her arms for a hug since she hadn't seen him for two days. Instead, Wayne held a chair for her at the worktable and sat across from her. A vein throbbed in his forehead.

"What's up, Wayne? You look as jolly as the couple in 'American Gothic.'"

"Juanita," he said with tensed jaw, "did I or did I not say I planned to leave Eddie Wagoner alone a while, then ask him again about Cooper's alibi?"

"You did. Of course."

"Then what did you think *you* were doing quizzing the kid?"

"Now, Wayne, I've known Eddie since he was little. I figured he'd open up to me when he wouldn't to you."

Wayne studied her like a drill sergeant momentarily nonplused by an uppity recruit's gall. Then he rose, spread his huge hands on the table and stuck his face close to hers.

"You couldn't resist poking your nose into my investigation, could you?"

She felt his warm breath on her cheek. This tough-guy behavior was too much. She had meant well, after all.

"If it had worked, you'd be thanking me."

"For interfering in my job? *Think again*." His face was florid, his voice cold. Fire and ice.

"And by the way, Juanita, exactly *what* were you doing peeking in windows last night at GIB COOPER'S PLACE?" He spat the last three words.

Oh, oh. She had thought he was too bent out of shape over one offense. It was two offenses.

"Someone who lived nearby called you?"

Abruptly Wayne sat down, as if weak with rage. She saw some other emotion struggle with anger in his face.

"Did you have to be so damned obvious about it? Asking questions of his neighbors? Prowling around outside his duplex? Driving a van that practically glowed in the dark?"

A corner of Wayne's mouth lifted, and she realized he was trying not to laugh. He conquered the urge, glowered at her again. She decided to meet the thaw part-way.

"Okay, I admit I shouldn't have looked in his window. Not that I saw anything important—just a bunch of stuff from the Vietnam War. But you see, Wayne, I have an advantage over you. I *know* Cooper was one of Asher's attackers. And I can't stand to see him still at large."

"You think I'm happy about it? That's a poor excuse for trespassing on private property. And none at all for messing into my case."

He had a point, but she couldn't bring herself to say so. Not when he hadn't even acknowledged her good intentions. Juanita gazed steadily at him, her mouth pressed together. He returned the look, equally tight-lipped. Two stubborn people, neither willing to back down.

Wayne rose, opened the door and strode out. Juanita heard

him tell Mavis goodbye. The front door opened and closed.

"Does this mean our date tonight is off?" she muttered.

She had been ready to tell him about the Nguyens' troubles, as well as the phone calls and the snake, but he had given her no chance. She sat staring into space, willing Wayne to come back, knowing he wouldn't.

To take her mind off the fight, she printed the alphabet forward, then backwards. Using this key, she filled in the cipher's remaining blanks. The message read:

> *We're on the move at last! Special unit*
> *to meet at the farm Tuesday at 10:00 p.m.*
> *   —The Major*

She had solved the mystery, but the code had been childishly obvious. Remembering Trevethan's snide comment about Katherine's cryptograms, Juanita felt glad he wasn't around to sneer. She poured more coffee and stood at the window drinking it. Rain fell lightly now, and the sky in the southwest had lightened.

The cipher was probably a kids' toy. But if not, what did it mean? Who was on the move? Doing what? "Special unit" and "The Major" suggested a military action. And where was the "farm" referred to? She sat again, wishing she could discuss the problem with someone. Ordinarily, she would call Wayne. That didn't sound like a great idea just now.

If this were the work of a local militia, it was an odd way to communicate. Perhaps its members were paranoid about phone wire-taps. Even then, would they use such an easy code? Still, from what she had read about such organizations, they sometimes did use crude, amateurish methods.

Assuming the note was serious, why had it been in Boston's returned book? Was the lawyer involved with the militia? Had he used the paper as a bookmark and left it absentmindedly, or could there be another reason for its being there?

When she had mentioned to him last evening finding something in his book, he had looked apprehensive, but had relaxed once she described the paper. What did that mean?

Staring at the blank computer monitor, Juanita tried to picture Boston as part of a paramilitary organization. She failed. She toyed with a scratchpad, flipping leaves back and forth. Would even a distracted reader use as a bookmark something as potentially explosive as the announcement of a secret meeting?

Maybe someone else had put the note in *The Shining*. But why? And who?

Juanita replayed in her mind the picture of Boston as he entered the library, puffing with exertion, greeting Meador and herself, handing his returns to the younger man.

Meador. What if the lawyer had intended to pass the cipher to him, as notice of a meeting he should attend? Uncomfortably, Juanita recalled Boston's surprised look when she had sent her assistant away and checked in the returned books herself.

Dismayed at the thought of her gentle young associate involved in something illegal or violent, she went to the glass again and looked out. The rain had stopped. The sky, though pewter overhead, was bright at the horizon. The storm was over.

One storm.

Chapter Eighteen

Ferris Asher died Friday.

When the news came over the local TV channel that evening, Juanita was standing at the sink tearing lettuce for a salad. The announcer recapped the church incident and said the minister had not regained consciousness following the attack. The funeral was to be Monday.

It seemed too much. On top of the worrisome events in town and her squabble with Wayne, now came the death of this good man. Juanita dropped onto a stool beside the counter, laid her head on her forearms and wept. At the sound Rip came from the dining room, tail waving gently, and laid a comforting paw on her leg.

As she was caressing him, she smelled something burning. Her supper! Juanita ran to the broiler, waved away a cloud of smoke and removed a blackened hunk of lemon-herb chicken breast. Assuring herself that less meat could only help the diet she had halfheartedly begun that morning, she cut off the worst charring and put it in Rip's bowl. He wolfed it as if it were a delicacy. Juanita finished her salad, made dry toast and ate mechanically, without enjoyment.

After supper she did laundry and vacuumed. But not even contemplating the living room's floor-to-ceiling bookcases and comfortable reading nooks cheered her as usual. She realized she was actually angry at herself. Even good intentions hadn't justified her conversations with Eddie. Had she swallowed her pride and admitted as much, Wayne and she could have made up. If he wasn't working tonight, they might now be at a movie or a restaurant in Tulsa.

Thinking of restaurants she liked, Juanita realized the frugal meal had not satisfied her. She needed something rich, something chocolate. Perched on a stool at the kitchen counter, she looked up a recipe for chocolate souffle. Immersing eggs in tepid water to warm them to room temperature, she got out utensils and measured ingredients.

Like the library reading room, her kitchen was a cherished spot, with spacious pecan cabinets, weathered brick on one wall and peach-and-ivory wallpaper on the others. Its size accommodated her whole gourmet club.

The egg whites fluffed nicely, and the concoction looked terrific going into the oven. Coming out, it tasted even better. She ate half, the chocolatey decadence sliding into a comforting pile in her stomach, and eyed the rest with regret.

Maybe she would visit Bach, see how the family were faring. But a look out the window at the dark house told her they weren't home. Then she recalled Bach mentioning a social tonight at the church that sponsored them. Perhaps Vivian Mathiesen would welcome a visitor. But Juanita's phone call to her home number got no answer. She decided not to try other friends, figuring she would be poor company anyway.

Curled in a wing chair in the living room with Rip languishing at her feet, Juanita tried to read a detective novel. After reading the same paragraph four times without comprehension, she abandoned it and turned on the television. However, sitcoms and sports programs seemed unrelated to a real life that included assaults on ministers, militia craziness, imbroglios over zoning, Eddie's troubles, Bach's anxieties—and Wayne's fury.

Finally Juanita went to bed. There, similar thoughts kept her awake till the wee hours.

Saturday she decided to stop moping and take positive action. Hoping to talk to Jenny again to learn if Walt had been home Monday evening, maybe even ask if his wife knew of a hate group in the area, she drove to the Fuller home.

Unfortunately, as she neared the white picket fence, Juanita saw a car in the drive, hood open, a heavy-set man bent over it. She drove on.

Entering the same downscale area where WRA had its headquarters, she stopped at an address she had looked up, a modest tan brick home. Clumps of yucca edged a driveway that held a showroom-sparkling red Cadillac. She got out and rang the doorbell. A potbellied man in jeans, plaid shirt and cowboy boots opened the door a few inches and looked inquiringly at her.

"Is this where Doyle Leggatt lives?" Juanita asked with a friendly smile.

"Yep. That's me."

Juanita explained she was the town librarian, researching a book on Wyndham's history, and asked to talk with him about land he had formerly owned.

"That new shopping center's bound to cause important changes in the area," she went on, "and I need some details about it for my book."

He paused, then opened the door wider.

"Come on in, ma'am. Don't know as I'll be any help. Can't say how the center'll change things. They ain't even started building it yet. But we can visit about it if you want."

They entered a living room with evidence of recently acquired wealth in obviously new overstuffed couches and lamps with shades still encased in plastic. A state-of-the-art videocassette receiver and a big-screen TV played a Gene Autry movie. Leggatt punched buttons on a remote, the film stopped and both appliances shut off.

"Actually, this is a long-term project," Juanita said, taking notebook and pen from her purse. "My research may take years. But I need to interview you now, while everything's fresh in your mind. You know, all about the rezoning fight and the various people involved."

"The rezoning, is it?" Leggatt took a meerschaum and a pipe tool from an ashtray on the coffee table. "You mind, ma'am? A pipe helps me think."

"Go ahead."

Leggatt ran the tool's prong around the inside of the pipe bowl, alternately grinning and frowning as if reliving a memory. He opened a glass humidor and dug the pipe into it.

"Well, what can I tell you?"

"Had you owned the property long? Before you got the offer to sell for a shopping center?"

"Not me, exactly. It belonged to my wife's people. She inherited it five years ago." Leggatt pushed tobacco into the bowl with a finger and tamped it lightly with the tiny spade. "She died a couple years later, and it was mine."

Juanita jotted notes in her book.

He put the stem in his mouth, struck a match and lit the pipe, drawing on it till a puff of smoke bloomed above him.

"We—her and me—talked about trying to develop it, sell off lots." He leaned back, savoring his smoke. "But we'd of had to go through a lotta red tape at city hall, then the lots might not sell good after all that. Land lies kinda low in that spot, y'know. Seems like people want those hillier lots like they got in northwest Wyndham." He took another drag, blew it out slowly. "Besides, the kids liked to play there, and they've used it ever since I can remember."

Juanita doodled a kitten face in the notebook margin. "But you sold it for the shopping center, so the kids can't use it any more anyway."

Leggatt's expression became part defensive, part sly. "Got to think of my old age, don't I? I like seeing kids have a place to play as much as anybody, but they offered me all that money, y'see."

Juanita drew a long-petaled sunflower. "Did you get flak from the neighbors when you applied for the rezoning? Did people call you names?"

"No. Mostly folks was okay. That little preacher got as hot as anybody, and he didn't even live around there."

"Ferris Asher?"

"Think that was it. Heard he got beat up last week—in his own church too." Leggatt shook his head as if unable to fathom such behavior.

"He died yesterday."

"Don't say." Leggatt drew on his pipe, produced a thread of smoke and stared thoughtfully at the TV. "That's too bad. I wouldn't of wished something like that on him."

"Even though he fought you over the rezoning?"

Leggatt looked shocked. "That's business. You don't wish real harm to people over a *business* deal."

The man was either incredibly naive or a terrific actor, Juanita thought.

"What about other people who wanted the zoning change? You think any of them wished harm to Rev. Asher?"

"Can't see why they would. Can't see why anybody would."

She decided he probably wasn't that good an actor.

"According to the paper, an Earl Trevethan argued strongly for the rezoning. He didn't have any personal interest in the outcome, did he?"

"Trevethan? Would he've been the old boy who did all the cussing?"

"Probably."

Leggatt chortled, gave the pipe's insides a poke with the prong. "He had a command of the language, I give him that. But no, not so far as I could see. 'Course you can't always tell what everybody's interest is, just from what they say." He drew forth a billow of smoke and nodded, satisfied.

"Take the banker. He talked against the zoning too. Acted like he just wanted the little kids to have their playground."

"Willard Pugh?" Juanita drew a sun, rays streaming across

the page.

"Think that was it." Leggatt grinned. "And all the time he had his own parcel to sell if my zoning got turned down."

Juanita nearly dropped the notebook. "Wait—you say Pugh backed Asher so he could sell property he owned?"

"Smart, huh? I bet most people didn't know that. But my lawyer—Boston—told me so."

Juanita jotted a note. So Pugh hadn't been disinterested after all. Had Trevethan had a hidden agenda too? Possibly even Ferris Asher?

Leggatt broke the silence. "Tell you something else Boston thought was going on. Only you can't put this in your book."

She waited expectantly.

"He figured there was some funny stuff with one guy on the council."

"What kind of 'funny stuff?'"

Leggatt rubbed a thumb and two fingers together, then pantomimed peeling dollar bills from a roll and placing them in Juanita's hand.

"Bribery?"

He nodded. "Boston wasn't sure, but he thought the corporation that was buying the land to build the center had bought off one council member. Piersall, him that's running for commissioner." Leggatt grinned. "'Course since it was helping our cause, we didn't raise a lot of questions.'"

Juanita tried to appear cool even as her pen flew over the paper. "Boston wasn't sure about it, you say?"

"Right. So you can't put that in. Okay?"

"I won't, unless I find it out from some source other than you." Juanita smiled reassuringly. She hadn't even thought of doing a book till that morning when searching for a cover story to explain her visit to Leggatt. Now she rather liked the idea. She had always loved research, especially uncovering little-known facts, not necessarily to publish them but just to hug information most others didn't have to herself. And a history of Wyndham would be a worthwhile contribution she could make to the town, something not everyone had the skills or determination to do.

If she did it, however, it couldn't be a puff piece. It must also include seamier goings-on, such as the bribery of a councilman, backed by proof far stronger than Leggatt's suspicions.

Besides, a truthful town history could answer that nagging question she had recently begun asking herself: Was Wyndham the idyllic little town she had once believed, or a far darker setting?

Chapter Nineteen

Sunday dragged for Juanita. She attended one of the town's several Baptist churches, where in the pastor's absence a ministerial student from a nearby denominational college occupied the pulpit. Though she sympathized with the "preacher boy's" nervousness, his faltering delivery and reliance on cliches made the sermon seem interminable. That afternoon she visited Bach, but the conversation proved dispiriting, both women distracted by worries. Juanita actually welcomed the start of another work week.

So did her assistants, evidently. Meador hummed softly as he checked in returns, and Mavis's scowl had retreated a degree since Friday. The Quote War renewed, but in such a benign form that the term "war" no longer seemed appropriate. Meador's offering said:

> *Wit is so shining a quality that everybody*
> *admires it; most people aim at it, all*
> *people fear it, and few love it except*
> *in themselves.*
> —Lord Chesterfield: *Letters to His Son,* July 21, 1752

Mavis replied:

> *Wit is folly unless a wise man hath the*
> *keeping of it.*
> —John Ray, *English Proverbs*

Juanita attended Ferris Asher's funeral that morning, entering the crowded Wyndham United Methodist Church sanctuary to see Wayne standing at the back with several other men. She spoke. He nodded coolly. Casting about for a seat, Juanita saw the Bromptons wave an invitation from a pew midway of the church. Gratefully she made her way up the aisle and into the space made for her. Cyril nodded solemnly, while a drawn-looking Eva wordlessly squeezed Juanita's hand.

Rev. Timothy Johnson, a gentle-faced pastor from Tulsa, spoke in a simple heartfelt way about his long-time friend Ferris Asher. But Juanita's mind wandered to the last time she had been in this room. On that Monday evening the scene had been poorly lit and chaotic, the furnishings upended and scattered. Now the lighting was bright, the Bible table, candelabra and high-backed chairs in their proper places, the ugly message on the wall painted over. Everything appeared ordinary save for the bronze casket flanked by masses of carnations, gladiolas and lilies.

Yet Juanita had the feeling she was overlooking something here, a clue unrecognized. What was she missing?

Her woolgathering ended abruptly as she realized the minister was talking about the fatal beating.

"Your pastor, my dear friend," he said, "lived a life that was all about love and tolerance. Yet ironically hatred and bigotry killed him."

Juanita stole a glance about her. The congregation sat quietly, with no coughing or rustling of paper. One woman had nodded off and was in danger of tumbling sideways. A young mother headed off her toddler's wail by popping a bottle nipple into his open mouth.

"The best memorial we could give Rev. Ferris Asher," Rev. Johnson went on, "would be to search our hearts and root out any malice we hold toward our fellow human beings."

Juanita's gaze lingered on an audience member in a nearby pew, a slightly built man in an ill-fitting brown suit, with a prominent Adam's apple and nearly non-existent lips. But it was his expression—part amusement, part defiance, part sneer, in contrast to the slightly pained look most people wore—that had made her pause. Juanita didn't recall seeing the man here before, though she was scarcely a regular herself.

After the service, mourners filed past the coffin, many openly weeping. Juanita's own eyes moistened as she gazed at Asher's translucent skin, his unnaturally straight mouth. She thought about people who would most feel his loss: his wife, church members he had inspired and counseled, Little Leaguers he had guided, community members he had befriended.

Anger flashed across her vision, a crimson blur. She turned and stumbled from the church.

Outside, people stood in knots, talking in hushed tones. Juanita joined the Bromptons and Bostons, who were church members here, and the Pughs, who were Episcopalians. All looked as sorrowful as she felt.

"A terrible thing," Willard Pugh said softly.

"Such a fine man to be so brutally killed," said Cyril. His bald head glistened with perspiration in the unseasonable warmth.

"And *young*," Estelle assented. "Too bad the day's so *muggy* and uncomfortable."

"A senseless killing." Eva wiped eyes red from crying.

"To us, yes." Roy Boston solemnly stroked his chin. "But it must've made some sort of sense to whoever did it."

"Must you always see the criminals' side, Roy?" said Mrs. Boston irritably. "This was a heinous act."

"Of course, dear. I was only pointing out—"

An awkward silence fell over them. Presently the man with the conspicuous Adam's apple paused in the church doorway, glanced around indecisively as if wondering whether to mingle, then walked away. His actions stirred a vague memory in Juanita.

"Who's that fellow?" she whispered to Eva.

It was Cyril who replied. "The little dark-haired guy?

He's been here the past several Sundays. Jeffcoat, his name is." He paused thoughtfully. "Sam Jeffcoat, I think."

"Shem," Boston said, eyes narrowing on Juanita's face. "Why do you ask about Shem Jeffcoat, Miss Wills?"

"No reason. I've seen him somewhere. Probably at the library."

"He used to farm around here," Boston added. "Lost his place a few years ago. Bitter about that, I hear—blames the government."

Just then Juanita noticed a rangy man with a bald head and bushy brows moving among the clusters of people, stopping at each to shake hands. Virg Piersall. When he reached her party and pumped flesh all around, she couldn't resist observing, "This must be a close race. Politicians don't usually work the crowds at funerals."

Piersall had the grace to look chagrined. "I'm not campaigning, Miss Wills. Rev. Asher was special to this whole community, and I came to pay my respects. He'll be sorely missed."

"Indeed he will."

Boston and the councilman glanced at each other, then away. Recalling their uneasy alignment during the zoning battle, Juanita wondered if the lawyer had voiced his bribery suspicion to his former ally. The candidate moved on, and she heard someone ask if he thought the defamatory poster would hurt his chances to win.

"Not at all," Piersall said cheerfully. "It seems to be helping, in fact. Voters don't like dirty tricks like that, you know."

Mariette Asher came out of the church with an elderly couple and a young man.

"Asher's parents and brother from Buffalo, New York," Eva Brompton murmured.

The four stopped just outside the door, and several mourners spoke words of condolence. Juanita lightly touched the widow's arm.

"I'm so sorry, Mariette. Ferris was a good man."

Mrs. Asher looked tiny and vulnerable in her severe black suit. Her face behind the wispy veil appeared puffy, but she managed a wavery smile.

"Thank you, Miss Wills. "And thanks more than I can say for helping Ferris that night. I was too preoccupied then—and at the hospital the other day—to tell you so."

"I wish I could've done more. Or that your husband's injuries hadn't been so bad."

Juanita watched the hearse lead away a procession the length of which would probably have surprised the modest Asher. She was about to walk back to the library when her eyes fell on Pugh's slight form. A thought struck her.

"Willard," she said, "would you have any time today to discuss a car loan?"

"I'll be in meetings all afternoon, but if you'll come on down now, we can talk."

"Great." Instead of returning to work, she went home and got her Chevy. It acted particularly stubborn when she started it this time, convincing her the loan discussion was happening none too soon.

At Federal National she waited briefly, then was shown to Pugh's inner sanctum, where he rose from behind a massive desk, his size and cherubic features at odds with his staid surroundings. The contrast reminded her of an unconvincing portrayal of Willy Loman she had seen in a high school production of "Death of a Salesman." Suppressing a chuckle, she took the chair Pugh waved her to. He sat facing her with a courteous, reserved gaze.

Having car-shopped earlier when the trading bug had first bitten, Juanita told him the type of car she wanted and how much she would need to borrow. They discussed rates and payment plans, then he swiveled to open a file drawer and take out a printed form.

"All right," he said, turning back, "let's get some figures and see what we come up with. Your income?"

She told him, then listed her monthly expenses. As Pugh recorded these, Cyril ducked in to drop two abstracts of title on a table. Pugh didn't look up. With a nod to Juanita, Cyril left. The application complete, Pugh leaned back, pushed his spectacles low on his nose and studied the figures.

"Looks good, Miss Wills. You have the wherewithal to repay the loan. We'll have to get a credit report, of couse, but I'm sure there'll be no problems." He laid the paper down, leaned closer and lowered his voice.

"You recall that rumor we were discussing the other evening? The one Estelle heard about 'orgies' at Darrow's farm? Well . . ." Pugh paused as if for effect. "I've since heard that same information from several others. Perhaps there's more to it than we thought."

"Have you been smoking Oklahoma's lucrative but illegal cash crop, Willard?"

Pugh regarded her unsmilingly. "Speaking of smoke, don't forget that old saying, 'Where there's smoke, there's fire.'"

"Juicy rumors spread faster around here than a couch potato's rear end, Willard. I hope you told those people you didn't believe this one."

"I don't actually know it's not true."

"You could give Doug the benefit of the doubt. As long as we're off the subject of my loan anyway, you weren't exactly candid with me about your part in the shopping-center zoning battle, were you?"

"Wasn't I?"

"You needed Leggatt's rezoning request to fail, so you could sell land of your own."

"Who told you that?"

"Is it true?"

Pugh's eyes twinkled behind his rimless glasses. He leaned back, hands behind head. "Yes and no. Estelle—or rather Estelle and her father—did own a tract that was being considered for the center. One that they've since sold for a very tidy sum. But *I* had no interest in the outcome. And I'm right about the traffic problem. You'll see."

"If Estelle profits, you profit. Sounds like a personal stake to me."

"You obviously don't understand how wheeler-dealers like Estelle's father operate. What they make on one deal goes immediately into another of my father-in-law's investments. I haven't seen a penny of their profit on that land."

Resenting his smirk, Juanita went on. "Another thing. You did go to City Council meeting last Monday, but you didn't stay the whole time, did you?"

"My, we're curious today, aren't we?" A smile played about his lips as if he found her increasingly amusing. "I left just after a zoning case I was interested in—I knew there'd be a battle over the annexed area's services and wasn't interested in that. Unlike Boston, I have no political ambitions, so I didn't have to try to court both sides in that mess. I came over to the bank and worked a while. Why do you care, anyway?"

She didn't answer.

All at once he giggled, a sound she didn't recall ever hearing him make before. "I see. Miss Sherlock is on the case, and she thinks I was one of those three masked men at the church." He let out a guffaw. "I can hardly wait to tell the others at Books."

Juanita felt her face grow warm. She could have handled this more subtly—speaking out of vexation was seldom a great idea. He chortled again, slapping the application form in his glee.

"You've given me a light moment in my day," he said when he regained control, "so I'll help you out this much.

From about ten-thirty Monday evening till the drugstore closed at eleven, I was there talking to the counter girl. Do check my alibi—I'm sure she'll back me up. Now, I must prepare for my meeting. We'll be in touch about that loan, but I wouldn't worry."

On leaving the bank, Juanita stopped in at the drugstore. She felt certain the banker's story would check out, but wanted to be thorough. The clerk, a frizzy-haired young woman with a vacant smile, did remember Pugh's being in last Monday.

"It's always a slow night, so at first I was glad to have somebody to talk to, even an old fart like him." With aid of a mirror behind the counter, she teased strands of her hair into a higher pouf. "I had to run him out when I was ready to lock up, though. He was strolling down memory lane about when he was a young guy just starting out."

Too bad, Juanita thought. She had begun to like the banker as a suspect. But if he had been here till eleven, he clearly couldn't have been at the church then, dressed in burglar's garb.

At least she had made headway in terms of trading cars.

Outside the drugstore, she paused. Nothing pressing awaited her at the library, and Okemah County Abstract Company was only two doors away.

Giving in to temptation, she walked over. No one was in the outer office, so she went on to Cyril's. When she entered, he was seated under a strong overhead light, desk piled high with abstracts and photocopies of documents. In his mirror-like crown, she saw an image of her own stocky body. Cyril's eyebrows lifted quizzically, but he said hello and asked her to sit down. She shut the door, sending his brows yet higher, and sat.

"So we meet a third time today, Juanita," he said, his green eyes friendly. "Can I help you in some way?"

"I hope so, Cyril. This is none of my business, but—it's just, well, I care about you and Eva, and this has been bothering me . . . ."

His eyes narrowed.

"What's the deal with you and that post office box in Lange's name?"

Cyril drew his breath in sharply.

"I mean, you said he's a neighbor, but Eva says you don't have a neighbor by that name. You don't have to explain, of course, but you know me, I can't resist prying . . . ." Realizing she was babbling, Juanita hushed. Silence followed. She fidgeted, one finger tracing a leaf design on her skirt, while Cyril stared out the window. When he spoke, his voice was so low she barely heard it.

"At least you didn't insist in front of Eva."

He continued gazing out the window, lower lip trembling, shoulders rigid. As she watched the obvious discomfort of a man she had known and liked all her life, guilt overcame Juanita's inquisitiveness. She rose to leave.

"Forget it, Cyril. I was way out of line in asking."

"Wait." The word was barely audible. When Juanita sat again, he went on. "I need to tell someone. You might do."

She waited, torn between sympathy and curiosity.

"You're a good friend, and somehow I think you'd understand better than my men pals. Besides, nosy as you are, you can keep a secret. But Eva mustn't ever find out. She'd be very hurt."

"Assuming it's not a matter for the police, I promise I won't tell anyone."

Removing a key ring from his pocket, he selected a key, inserted it in a bottom desk drawer and took out a stack of magazines. He paged through one and spread a photo layout in front of Juanita.

Nude pictures she had seen in *Penthouse* and *Playgirl* had neither shocked nor especially titillated her, but these had a sinister quality, coupling violence with sexuality. Men and women appeared in demeaning poses, bestial tormentors forcing them to abuse each other. She blushed for Cyril. Watching her, he colored too.

"I know," he said. "I don't understand it myself."

"So you rented that box in a fake name to keep your wife from finding out you were receiving this material."

He nodded. "Eva sometimes picks up our personal mail, and the secretary gets what comes to the office."

"Is it legal to send that stuff through the mail?"

"I think so, though it comes in plain wrappers with a box-number return address. Anyway, it's my business, no one else's."

A thought occurred to Juanita. "Does Willard Pugh know? Is that why he teased you about importing your excitement?"

Cyril looked sheepish. "I think he saw one of my magazines when he was here one day. He'll probably never say for sure, just keep dropping embarrassing hints. At least you came right out in the open."

Juanita didn't speak for a time, pondering the revelation. At last she said, "I need to ask something else, Cyril. That awful poster about Virg Piersall—did you have anything to do with putting it out?"

His eyes widened. "You think I . . . Juanita! Oh, I see, because of these pictures. I promise you, I had nothing to do with that."

"If I imagined you'd try to practice any of that stuff on a vulnerable child or a woman—"

"I'd cut my own hands off first." His quiet intensity, the directness of his gaze, convinced her.

"I'm not the thought police, Cyril. And I did promise not to tell Eva. But you might want to. She's a pretty understanding woman."

"She doesn't deserve to be burdened with this."

Juanita soon took her leave, but decided to check something else before leaving downtown. Walking to Roy Boston's ground-floor law office, she entered the outer room and found a bored-looking young woman at a desk filing her fingernails, an encouraging sign the boss might be out.

"Is Mr. Boston here?" Juanita asked in a hopeful tone.

"Sorry. He's in court."

Juanita feigned disappointment, started to leave, then turned back. "Actually, you can probably help me. I found this in a book he returned to the library, and was wondering if he'd missed it." She took the cipher from her bag and held it out.

The secretary flipped reddish-brown curls over her shoulder and glanced at the paper without interest. "Doesn't mean anything to me."

"Could it have gotten in the book some other way?" persisted Juanita, warming to her role of officious public servant. "Maybe someone put it there as a joke? I wouldn't want to throw it away if it's important."

The young woman shrugged. "Maybe one of his kids stuck it in there at home."

"How about here? Would he leave the library books somewhere in this office till he returned them?"

"Usually on that cabinet—" The secretary indicated a filing cabinet near the front door, then drew back her hand. "Why'd you ask that? The paper didn't come from this office. If somebody put it in Mr. Boston's book, it's their problem if they've lost it."

Juanita thanked her and left, musing that someone who knew the attorney's library habits could have come in when the secretary was away from her desk and placed the note in *The Shining*. Cyril, for instance. An abstracter's presence in a law office would be routine, as in a bank.

None of that mattered, however, unless the bookmark was

evidence of some crime. As far as she knew, it wasn't.

Approaching her auto, she pressed the button on her remote. After a false start or two, the car responded on cue, headlights springing to life, siren chirping. But using Wayne's gift plunged her into gloom. If only they hadn't had that argument. If only Wayne weren't so touchy. Or if only she had admitted . . .

"If wishes were horses," she muttered, "I wouldn't have had to keep the blasted Chevy this long."

Chapter Twenty

When Juanita returned to the library, she found a note to call Vivian Mathiesen. She phoned the newspaper office.

"I thought if you hadn't eaten lunch yet, we might have a late lunch together," said Vivian's gravelly voice. "I haven't time for the Coachman, but if you don't mind the Dog 'n' Suds how about meeting me there?"

Juanita had brought a sack lunch, but decided it would keep until tomorrow. "Sure. But if you're following up on what we talked about last week, I don't have anything to give you."

Vivian's reply was a throaty laugh, followed by a spasm of coughing. "You're a suspicious one, Juanita. Can't two friends simply have lunch together?"

"If you say so. Fifteen minutes from now?"

"Perfect."

In the crowded fast-food restaurant, Vivian commandeered the one available booth. Just as she and Juanita picked up their food and sat down, Wayne and another policeman came in. They placed an order and looked around for a place to sit. The other officer, a slender blond who looked as if he should be eating at the junior-high cafeteria, called a greeting to Vivian and came over.

"Look who's here. Hey, ladies, can we join you? All the other tables are full."

"Hi, Bob. Juanita Wills, meet Bob Whitlow, my neighbor. Sure, join us. Okay with you, Juanita?"

She nodded reluctantly, and he sat beside Vivian. Soon Wayne carried a tray to the booth, said a reserved hello and stood awkwardly in the aisle. Juanita greeted him distantly, but moved over. He perched on the booth's outside edge. It seemed a toss-up which was more uncomfortable.

Bob and Vivian talked about the weather and the community college basketball team's winning season. Typically a fast eater, Wayne appeared to be trying to break his own record. Then Vivian raised the topic Juanita had dreaded.

"You making any progress on the Asher case, Wayne?"

He shrugged his burly shoulders, avoiding Juanita's eyes. "You can report we're following up leads and carrying out a full investigation."

Vivian grinned at the evasion. "Off the record, Detective Cleary, you going to be able to solve it?"

"Off the record, I'm not sure."

"Juanita hasn't cracked it for you yet? She was giving me the third-degree last week about people she suspected. I figured she'd have solved it by now."

My friend, Vivian Mathiesen, Juanita thought.

Irritation flamed in Wayne's eyes as he looked directly at Juanita for the first time. But he said calmly, "That right? I guess she's been holding out on me."

Juanita tried for a light tone. "Vivian's kidding, Wayne. I was just wondering aloud to her about whether Asher might have made lasting enemies in the shopping-center zoning fight, that's all."

He gave her a long steady look, then resumed eating.

But Vivian couldn't let it rest. Waving a French fry drenched in catsup, she said teasingly, "Juanita suspects lots of folk, including some very prominent men in town. But I guess in an investigation you have to be suspicious of everybody, right, Detective?"

"You'd have to ask Miss Wills about that," Wayne said evenly. "I tend to suspect the people with motive and/or opportunity. But then she's not hampered by having had police-academy training like I am." He swallowed a bite of hot dog and tossed his napkin on the table. "Let's hit it, Bob. 'Scuse us, ladies."

Bob bolted the remaining third of his sandwich, said his goodbyes and followed Wayne out, leaving Juanita relieved though sad. Sitting so close to Wayne, smelling his scent but being emotionally at war, had been subtle torture. She told herself it might be better if they broke up for good. Wayne could be snide at times, witness that police-academy remark. She also didn't like his job's odd hours and potential danger.

Besides, he was pig-headed. The fact she was too was beside the point.

Vivian broke into her reverie. "What's with you and Wayne? Have a fight or something? He wasn't his usual easy-going self."

"We did, as a matter of fact. You didn't help a lot, talking about me solving his case for him."

"Oh, I get it. He doesn't appreciate your input."

"You might say that."

"Sorry, kid. By the way, I got curious about Gib Cooper since you were so interested in him, and sounded out one of his co-workers at the computer place."

"And?"

"She's afraid of him. Said he doesn't make friends with others, just keeps to himself. And the way he looks at her makes her nervous."

"Tell me about it."

"You afraid of him too? Why?"

"Not now. Maybe I'll fill you in some day."

"There's more." Vivian rolled her tongue around her upper teeth, working food loose. "She told me Cooper grew up here. He doesn't talk a lot about himself, but did mention that much. So I looked up Mrs. Schlesinger, a retired high school teacher I know. Her mind's still laser-sharp, and she remembered Cooper well." Vivian balled her napkin and tossed it on her plate.

"So? Your pregnant pauses are annoying, Viv."

"Seems he was always getting into scrapes. His folks were good people, but couldn't handle their son. It eased their minds when he joined the army."

"What kind of scrapes?"

"Lifting cars for joy-rides, burning down a vacant house, putting a loaded pistol in another kid's locker at school. They could never prove anything, but he was always in the vicinity when such things happened. Mrs. Schlesinger said he was bound to get caught in something he couldn't talk his way out of."

"His folks still live around here?"

"Dad's dead, mother's in a nursing home. Mind's gone."

Juanita offered Vivian the rest of her fries. She declined.

"Changing the subject, Viv, I heard Roy Boston has political aspirations. You know anything about that?"

Vivian chuckled. "Not specifically, but lawyers generally do, don't they? Roy's cultivated some powerful people over the years. And some shady ones."

"Shady? Like whom?"

"Again, I don't know specifics. But he's defended people rumored to have ties to big-time drug interests." She shook her head. "Forget I said anything. It's just gossip."

Juanita hesitated. "Speaking of gossip, I heard some—unfounded, I'm sure. Don't pass it on, okay?" She told what Estelle Pugh had said about Doug.

Vivian nodded. "A guy at the paper heard Darrow's supposedly hosting crack parties for high school kids."

"You believe the story?"

"Nope. A teacher'd have to be a complete fool to risk that. Darrow may be many things, but a fool he's not."

"Still, if the story's getting around town. . . ."

"It's his problem, Juanita. You can't fix everything. Incidentally, I asked Piersall's campaign manager about that poster. He claimed not to know who'd done it, but didn't seem nearly as pissed off about it as I'd have expected. Well, I gotta get out of here—dying for a smoke."

They left. In spite of the confrontation with Wayne, Juanita thought, lunch had been productive. Thanks to Vivian, she now knew more about Gib Cooper.

Nothing that in any way reassured her, however.

Chapter Twenty-one

On the way home that evening, Juanita reached a decision. She felt sure Eddie was somehow tied in with Asher's attackers, so if he wouldn't admit the truth she would find it out another way. He had told Doug he was off work Monday evenings but was always busy then. And Asher had been assaulted last Monday, the evening for which the boy had alibied Cooper. It seemed at least a possibility that whatever Eddie did on Mondays also involved the computer repairman.

She would follow the teenager tonight.

Trying not to think about Wayne's reaction if he should find out, she made a sandwich and a thermos of coffee. Her phone rang and she answered, but heard only breathing at the other end. Oh no, she thought with a shiver of dread.

"Quit horning in where you don't belong, lady," the now-familiar whisper said, "or you'll be mighty sorry." The tone was more menacing than before, the speaker still unidentifiable.

With shaking hand, Juanita replaced the receiver. If she were to tell Wayne about the calls now, with things as they were between them, would he even believe her? She told herself anonymous phone calls were made by cowards who wouldn't dare carry out their blustering threats. But she felt decidedly nervous. Sending unsigned letters also showed lack of courage, yet the Nguyens' harasser had acted on his hatred.

Dressed in sweatshirt, jeans and running shoes in case the surveillance should involve walking, Juanita drove to the Wagoner service station. Eddie's Ford was the only vehicle in sight, so Bud must be at supper. She parked down the block where she had a good view of the station, feeling excited but a little silly.

"Librarians don't do a lot of stakeouts," she muttered,

settling back in her seat.

Ten minutes later, Bud's brown pickup turned in. He got out and went into the station. Then Eddie appeared, climbed into his Fairlane and peeled out. With Juanita following at a cautious distance, he drove to a seedy part of East Wyndham where defunct appliances occupied sagging porches and where rusty autos and car parts littered yards. Eddie stopped in front of a large house with bright yellow paint. Juanita recognized the black Gremlin parked in the driveway as Edith Wagoner's. She parked a few houses away and waited.

Minutes dragged by. Juanita read everything readable on dash and gearshift, then poured half a cup of coffee and drank it. Immediately, she wished she hadn't. If this should turn into a long night of waiting, she would regret every drop of liquid in her bladder.

The door of the Wagoner house remained shut. She opened her sandwich, tore bits off and chewed them, crumpled the wrapper and returned it to its sack. She read the dashboard markings again. Would this be the one Monday Eddie would stay home?

But after three-quarters of an hour, he came out. They drove off again, he with a lurch and squealing of tires, she with a prayer the Chevy wouldn't fail her.

At first he seemed to drive aimlessly, turning north, west, south, east, north again and so on. She had about decided he was joy-riding and was ready to give up when he came to the west edge of town and picked up speed. Had he opened up the Ford he probably could have easily left her behind, but he kept to the speed limit. Seven miles from town they passed Doug Darrow's residence, where she and Wayne, parched from horseback-riding, had once stopped to ask for a drink.

Something seemed to be happening at the Darrow property tonight. She slowed to look. Three pickups stood under a blazing yard light. Two young men walked toward the farmhouse, while another male adolescent called a greeting from the open kitchen door. Was this one of the infamous "orgies" she had heard about?

Yeah, right. But *something* was going on.

Five miles beyond Doug's place, with Juanita hanging well back to avoid being spotted, Eddie abruptly slowed and turned right. He sailed through an open steel gate, bounced over a cattle guard onto a graveled road, gunned the Ford and disappeared behind a spume of dust. Signs saying "Posted—no hunting" hung at intervals along a heavy wire fence.

Juanita drove beyond the gate, continued a hundred yards and turned. She again passed the entrance, searching for evidence of habitation, seeing none. The moon was high now, the sky sprinkled with stars. The graveled road ran through a pasture broken on the right by a creek edged with brush and saplings. Some 200 yards along the road, a dense stand of timber loomed.

Uncertain what to do, Juanita continued driving past the entrance. She would have liked to follow Eddie but had no idea what she would be getting into. Peeking into Cooper's window when he was out was one thing. Driving onto strange land uninvited, maybe blundering into something someone would kill to keep secret, was another. In her mind, she heard the anonymous caller's warnings.

As she was nearing the gate headed toward Wyndham, an ancient rust-mottled green pickup approached from the direction of town, reaching the entrance just before she did. The vehicle braked suddenly, slid around the turn and through the posts. As it made the corner, her car lights revealed the driver, a small dark man with a prominent Adam's apple. She had the feeling she had seen him somewhere recently.

Then she remembered. The man at Asher's funeral. What had Cyril and Boston called him? Shem Jeffcoat.

Intrigued, Juanita slowed and pulled onto the shoulder, watching as the pickup gained speed. Like Eddie's car, it disappeared in a powdery haze.

All at once she realized something about Jeffcoat. He could be Teeny Guy. Not only was he the right size, but his hesitation in the church doorway today recalled how T.G. had paused in that same spot. Also, if the painted hate message had been a response to the minister's preaching, someone must have monitored his sermons. Jeffcoat, perhaps. Juanita had already decided not to drive up that graveled road, but this new awareness crystallized that decision.

Perhaps she should tell Wayne. But he wouldn't be convinced by her suspicions, and she couldn't follow Jeffcoat in search of proof.

Noting her speedometer reading to check the mysterious property's distance from Wyndham, Juanita headed back toward town. When she again passed Darrow's place, two autos had joined the vehicles under the yard light.

Half a mile beyond the farmhouse, she met Meador's red Ford Escort. Still wondering what was happening up that graveled road, she barely registered the car's passage.

Maybe Eddie's secret Monday activity was something as simple as hunting with friends on posted land. But would they do that every Monday? She wondered if the farm referred to in Boston's bookmark was out this way. At least she knew Eddie hadn't gone to the meeting mentioned, which was to be on a Tuesday.

Then she recalled passing Meador's car. Had he been going the same place as Eddie? Juanita fought rising panic, telling herself her assistant was probably just on his way to Tulsa or to visit a friend who lived in this direction.

But she needed to know.

Juanita braked, reversed and drove as fast as safety allowed after him. She went past the Darrow property, then the steel gate, and ten miles beyond. But unless Meador had speeded up dramatically, he had turned off somewhere.

"Not necessarily the same place Eddie and Jeffcoat did, though," she insisted aloud. She heard a thumping sound. "Great, now I've got a flat."

Noticing a turn-off to the right, apparently the end of a long driveway, she turned into it, stopped and got out. She was lifting the spare from her trunk when a fawn-colored Buick Riviera came down the drive, slowed and stopped. Roy Boston got out, wearing khaki pants, windbreaker, dress shoes and a gimme cap from a well-servicing outfit.

"Having trouble, Miss Wills?" he called heartily. "Let me help." He took the jack from Juanita's trunk, fitted it under the Chevy's bumper, loosened the flat's lug nuts and hoisted the car off the ground. All the while he chattered about the fine evening and the less-than-fine condition of her car. "What is this, a '90 or '91? You've got more confidence in it than I'd have. Wouldn't want my wife driving at night in a clunker like this, not out away from town." He removed the tire and inspected it critically.

"Actually it's been a pretty good car, till lately. I guess I haven't paid enough attention to the tires, though."

"This one's practically bald. What brought you out here tonight anyway?" He settled the spare in place.

"I felt like a drive. As you say, it's a nice evening. But I might ask the same question of you. How do you happen to be out here?"

"Brooding about a case. The fellow who owns this land lets me come out and trudge through his woods when I want to." He tightened the nuts, lowered the car, loaded the flat and jack in her trunk and dusted off his hands. "That should get you back to town."

She thanked him, crawled in the Chevy and turned it around. As she reached the end of the drive and paused to check traffic on the main road, she noticed a mailbox on a wooden post at the roadside. It bore a rural box number and the name "Jesse Shipman."

Virg Piersall's opponent in the county commission race. So Boston was friends with the councilman's political rival.

She thought about that the rest of the way home. Boston had earlier said he liked to walk in the country to think, but he had also claimed to wear military boots when doing so. He had been wearing dress shoes tonight. Maybe his reason for being here had more to do with Shipman's campaign than with hiking?

If so, why didn't Boston want his support of the politician known?

Chapter Twenty-two

Eddie bumped along the graveled road, relishing the feel of the steering wheel in his hands. It felt great to be away from the job, his parents and school, with just his Fairlane for company. Some guys called it an old people's car, but at least he could work on it himself, not like with today's computerized jobs.

He entered a tall thick stand of trees. Some varieties hadn't leafed out yet, but luxuriant evergreens darkened the passage even in daylight. They also blocked highway noise, giving the lane a restful quality. Eddie thought of the forest as a tunnel to another world—one of men and important plans, where he was capable, appreciated.

He turned the wheel a little to the right, grinning at the Ford's instant response. He wished he had more chances to test it out. The folks kept a tight rein on him. Even on Mondays and Thursdays, his nights off, they demanded to know where he went. But he and Joey had worked out a system for Mondays, claiming each week to be at a movie or working on a school project together.

Mondays weren't really nights off, not with the Major issuing rules for everything, including the way they traveled to and from meetings. Eddie wasn't to drive a straight route from his house to the farm, nor to go above the speed limit.

"Don't call attention to yourself," the Major's dictum went.

In that respect G.O.L. seemed like school, where somebody was always telling Eddie what to do. At least he had gotten offers of help with his studies lately, even if Miss Wills' notion of assistance was to arrange that dreaded interview. Maybe lightning would strike him dead first, or the world would end tonight.

His gloom lightened as he entered a clearing and pulled

into a space among some twenty cars on a dirt parking lot to the left of the frame house G.O.L. used as headquarters. A board sidewalk led from parking lot to office. Dense undergrowth hugged the structure's rear and right side. Through brush behind the house, Eddie could see drop-lights hanging on the wooden barn and metal Quonset hut that housed weapons.

He remembered his first meeting. Gib had proudly showed him around, pointing out training areas: the firing range, the arena for hand-to-hand combat and the long rolling stretch of terrain Eddie had traversed to reach the machine-gun nest last week. And over everything like a green canopy, the dense woods.

"Perfect, ain't it?" Gib had bragged. "Even from the air you can't see or hear nothing."

Eddie now followed a well-worn path from parking lot to barn, reaching it as Gib came out cradling a machine gun.

"Hey, Sport," he said, "how's it going?"

"Okay." Eddie hesitated. "Well, mostly okay. That cop come back and asked if I was sure it was Monday you and me was together."

Gib's eyes became slits. He set the gun down.

"'Course I said yes," Eddie added hastily. "You can depend on me, Gib."

The older man studied the younger keenly. Apparently satisfied, he clapped him on the back. "I know I can, Eddie. You just stay cool and don't volunteer nothing." He grinned. "Words to live by, Eddie: never volunteer, never explain."

Eddie nodded. He had never been the volunteering type anyway. "It ain't just the police, Gib. Miss Wills knows I wasn't with you Monday. She's been bugging me to tell the truth."

"So? You don't owe her nothing, kid. Ignore her."

"Yeah, Gib. Only . . ."

The steely gray eyes bored into Eddie. "Only what?"

"Well, she was kind of nice to me when I was a kid. And she's helping me with a English paper I got to write. I sort of feel bad about lying to her, Gib."

Gib's demeanor changed. He grabbed Eddie by his collar, yanked him close and gripped his shoulders like a vice. Eddie smelled citrus aftershave and tobacco. He had never noticed before how hard Gib's eyes looked when he got mad, like shiny gray metal. This wasn't the teasing, boastful big-brother Gib he knew. It was a person whose existence Eddie had guessed at but had never confronted.

"You're not going to tell her, kid." Even the voice had a metallic quality, tough and cold as iron. "You're not going to tell nobody. Got that? You understand me?" He shook Eddie till the boy thought his bones should clank.

"Sure, Gib. I didn't mean I was planning to tell her. I can handle her, Gib. You can count on me." Even as he placated his hero, Eddie felt resentment rise in him. Gib ought to know by now he could trust him.

The painful grip relaxed. Gib stepped back, grinning. "We had a good time spooking the gooks the other night, didn't we, kid?"

Eddie nodded. He actually felt uncomfortable about what they had done, but wasn't about to tell Gib so. He went into the storage barn and helped carry out equipment. So far he didn't feel the excitement a meeting night usually brought, but figured he would once the Major began talking.

When the members were assembled in battered metal folding chairs in the briefing room, largest of the house's four rooms, the Major stood at a chalkboard facing them. Though his hair was graying, his once-powerful chest sagging, he still cut an impressive figure with his shoulders braced military-fashion, his expression discouraging excuses. As he spoke of the necessity to be so well prepared that in battle each man would do his job instinctively, he wove his usual spell over Eddie.

He described the evening's exercise, a variation on previous machine-gun drills. Eddie's adrenaline pumped, but he listened carefully. Unsureness in the field could get him hurt or killed.

The Major and Gib accompanied the troops to the course and saw the exercise begin as usual, but this time left a lieutenant in charge and went back to the office. Eddie had no time to worry about their absence, however, as he concentrated on following orders and maintaining his excellent training record.

When he had finished, he felt a rush of happiness in a job expertly done, the feeling he lived for these days. He also had a powerful thirst from dust kicked up on the course. So instead of waiting for Joey as usual, Eddie went back alone to headquarters, where a large canister of water stood on a table outside.

As he twisted the spigot, running liquid into a paper cup, he heard voices through an open rear window. That would be the command center, the War Room as the Major called it.

Curious, Eddie eased over and looked inside. Gib and the Major stood at a desk, intent on their conversation. To one side, a third man's uniformed leg was visible.

"I tell you, it's time to do something about Wills," Gib said. "She came snooping around my place the other night. The old geezer next door told me so." He thrust his thumbs into his fatigue pants' waistband and stuck his chest out combatively. "Now she's working on the kid. Nosy bitch deserves a good lesson."

The Major eyed Gib coldly. "If that means you want to harm her, maybe even kill her, forget it. We already have the cops' attention thanks to you, Cooper. We can't afford more right now." He set his fists on his hips. "You kept saying the preacher needed a warning too, and you see how that got out of hand. I should've never listened to you."

Shaking his head in disgust, the Major shoved an unlit pipe into his mouth and began striding up and down the small room, reminding Eddie of General MacArthur in a movie he and Joey had seen. The teen drew back, fearing his superior might glance in his direction.

"All the books say intimidate by fear," the Major spoke around the pipe, "and keep actual violence to a minimum till you're trained and ready to move militarily." He reached a wall and swiveled for the return trip.

"The *books*," Gib hooted.

The third man spoke, unintelligibly. As stealthily as he ever moved in training, Eddie edged to the other side of the window. Now he recognized the small dark man, the one they called Jeffcoat. The Major stopped in front of Gib and glared at him.

"While we're on the subject of laying low, Cooper, I heard you tell one of the other men about hassling some slant-eyes in town. That true?"

Gib spat toward a corner of the room. "I may've had to put up with gooks in 'Nam, but I don't have to live around them here."

"That's not a G.O.L.-sanctioned project, Cooper." The Major's voice held suppressed fury. "A couple Vietnamese don't amount to anything. But your bothering them could jeopardize our real operations. Lay off."

"What's the big deal? A nasty note and some garbage on their porch. They can't possibly know who did it."

"The big deal is that a letter sent through the mail could bring in the Feds. And somebody may've seen you toss that garbage out. I said stop it. NOW."

Gib finally rumbled what sounded like assent. Eddie moved away. He had found the conversation fascinating, but wished he hadn't heard it. Especially Gib's talk about Miss Wills, like he wanted to murder her, partly because Eddie had mentioned her asking him questions.

If only he didn't have to grow up, deal with adult problems. When he was little and his mother dragged him everywhere like extra baggage, he had thought he couldn't wait to get big. Now he recalled such times with longing.

Chapter Twenty-three

Tuesday, the Quote War escalated dramatically. Meador fired the opening shot:

Said John, Fight on, my merry men all,
I am a little hurt, but I am not slain;
I will lay me down for to bleed a while,
Then I'll rise and fight with you again.
—*The Ballad of Johnnie Armstrong*

The sudden switch from peaceful subjects like learning and wit to fighting puzzled Juanita.

And Mavis, it seemed. She went about morning duties distractedly or sat at the counter staring into space, her hands oddly unbusy. But at last she replied:

He that fights and runs away
May live to fight another day.
—Anonymous

Juanita happened to be in the office when Meador read it. "Pitiful," he muttered. Minutes later, he responded:

Every man thinks meanly of himself
for not having been a soldier.
—Samuel Johnson, in *Boswell's Life*

Mavis rallied with:

A soldier is a Yahoo hired to kill in
cold blood as many of his own species,
who have never offended him, as possibly
he can.
—Jonathan Swift: *Gulliver's Travels IV. u*

"That's more like it," Meador said with relish. He countered:

Might is right; justice is the interest
of the stronger.
        —Plato: *Republic I. xii.*

"'Might is right?'" Juanita asked disbelievingly as he tacked it to the wall. He raised his eyebrows enigmatically and left the office.

Later Juanita joined her assistants in the reading room and noticed Mavis sneaking surreptitious looks at Meador. After he had loaded the returns cart and gone to the stacks to shelve books, Juanita broached the subject.

"What's come over Meador lately? He's acting strange."

Mavis snorted with something like her old fire. "He's always been a lazy brat. What's different?"

Juanita rolled her eyes upward. "You know what I mean, Mavis. This sudden militaristic turn."

"I guess you haven't seen him back in the stacks lately, shadow-boxing and doing karate kicks."

"Meador? No kidding."

Mavis nodded triumphantly. "I'd have mentioned it before, but you'd have called it tattling. You always take his side."

Actually Juanita had seen Meador in the stacks yesterday flipping through a book on martial arts. But since he often scanned returns he was shelving, she had thought nothing of it. Now she wondered again about seeing him last evening. If a paramilitary group really was active locally, and if Meador had gotten mixed up with it, that might explain this new pugilistic attitude. The thought troubled her.

She was sitting at her desk, wondering if she should ask him where he had been going, when the phone rang. It was

Estelle Pugh.

"Juanita," she said exasperatedly, "this is *most* annoying. I *must* ask you to trade *shifts* with me."

"Oh? Why?" Juanita didn't attempt to disguise her lack of enthusiasm. She had gotten used to driving Thursdays.

"We've *lost* one of our *grants*," the grating voice continued, "so I *must* tape a plea for *funds*. I called the TV station to arrange a *time*, but they didn't call *back* till after I'd *left* yesterday." She sighed heavily. "Willard—I swear, men can be so *infuriating*—Willard *thoughtlessly* agreed I'd do it next *Monday* afternoon. Well, there's *no* way I can tape a spot in Tulsa, with *Lord knows* how many retakes, and get back in time to do my *shift*. He didn't think how *tight* it would make my schedule, he said."

"Maybe one of the other drivers—" Juanita began.

Estelle cut her off. "Juanita, there's *no one* else. I've asked them all *before*. People get *used* to a schedule and *refuse* to change. They all have some *excuse*, of course."

"Is that right?" Juanita searched her own brain for a plausible demurrer.

"I even thought of getting *Willard* to drive my shift, but he has a *lodge* committee meeting next Monday. You've *got* to help me."

Finding her subterfuge mechanism on the fritz, Juanita reluctantly agreed. Estelle would drive Thursday this week, and Juanita would do both Monday and Thursday next week.

As she hung up, Mavis sauntered into the office, taped a paper on the quote wall and left again. Juanita read:

> *Justice is too good for some people*
> *and not good enough for the rest.*
> —Norman Douglas: *Goodbye to Western Culture*

It wasn't directly responsive to Meador's last contribution, but Juanita saw the problem. He had introduced a new element into the battle, and Mavis was having trouble shifting gears.

He came in shortly thereafter, looked perplexed as he read the new quote, but said nothing. Soon he added another:

The art of war . . . I take to be the highest
perfection of human knowledge.
—Daniel Defoe: *Introduction to The History of Projects*

Later, when Meador and Juanita were seated together at the circulation desk, she asked, "What's with all this stuff about war and fighting, Meador? If your plan is to drive Mavis out of her mind, it seems to be working."

Meador squared his shoulders. "I'm just sick of being a doormat. If Mavis has a hard time with that, too bad."

"But what brought this on?" Juanita spun a pencil, noticed its point was dull and took it to a sharpener fastened to a near-by pillar. "I liked the old Meador. He was nice to be around, and certainly not a doormat."

"Maybe you haven't noticed since you're hefty yourself, but I'm fat and soft. Even little guys think they can push me around."

"Watch the 'hefty' remarks." Juanita twisted the handle too hard, and the pencil point snapped. "Some people are jerks, Meador. You don't have to emulate them."

"Easy for you to say—you're not a guy. A few weeks ago as I was coming out of a movie, a bunch of punks came up and started hassling me." Meador's round cheeks flushed. "I think they'd have beat me up if a cop car hadn't come by. But I'm not taking that stuff any more."

Juanita turned the crank carefully, thinking about this changed attitude. She had always taken Meador's mildness for granted, as she had Mavis's irritability. She returned to her stool.

"I saw you last night out west of town," she said lightly. "Driving to Tulsa, were you?"

He rubbed at an imaginary spot on the counter. "No, just went for a drive. Nice evening, wasn't it?"

Juanita agreed it had been. Meador dug in a pocket of his vest sweater, brought out a bag of lychee nuts and offered them. She declined. He opened and ate one.

"I see you've picked up Doug's habit."

"These things grow on you."

"I suppose."

Mavis came out of the office and, not glancing at her colleagues, began tidying away books left on an alcove table. As one, Meador and Juanita went to read the new quote. It said:

Peace hath her victories
No less renowned than war.
—John Milton: *To the Lord General Cromwell*

"You ought to be ashamed," Juanita said. "You've broken her spirit."

Meador grinned. "She's bound to have something better up her sleeve. She's just setting me up for a real assault."

"You're probably right. But even as a tactic in war, I find the notion of Mavis as peacemaker pretty startling."

Planning to use her lunch hour to check on the mysterious farm's ownership, Juanita phoned a friend in the county treasurer's office. "Lena, how would I find out who owns a piece of real estate a few miles outside town but still in the county?"

"Got the legal? I can tell you who pays taxes on it."

Juanita said she didn't know the land's legal description, only how many miles it was from Wyndham.

"Okay, go to the assessor's office. They've got a big map of the county, and they can help you figure out the legal."

In the assessor's office Juanita found the location of the farm on an age-darkened map on the wall. The name "Jeffcoat" was lettered across the large square.

"That map hasn't been updated for years," a smiling clerk told her, "so the tract you're interested in may've changed hands." She worked out the needed legal description for Juanita and sent her to the county clerk's office, where she learned Federal National Bank had foreclosed on the property. It had been sold at sheriff's sale to a corporation, Security Enterprises Inc. Roy Boston had represented the bank in the foreclosure action.

"Do you have information on this corporation?" Juanita asked an employee. "Corporate address and officers' names?"

The staffer checked another book, then shook her head. "It must not be incorporated here. Maybe in one of the surrounding counties. You could call each of the county clerks and ask."

Juanita left the courthouse, thinking that phoning a bunch of clerks around the state sounded like a pain. But she had made a good start. The property in question must be the farm whose loss had made Jeffcoat bitter against the government, according to Boston. Roy would have reason to know, she thought, since he had helped to take the land away.

And now Jeffcoat had been seen entering his former farm. With or without the current owners' permission?

When Juanita reached the library, another idea occurred to her. In the reference room she learned from the Oklahoma Statutes that all companies doing business in Oklahoma had to register with the Secretary of State. She wrote to that office asking for information on Security Enterprises Inc., printed the letter and was proofreading it when Mavis said someone was asking for her at the front desk. Correspondence in hand, Juanita went to the reading room.

There, an elderly woman she had helped to find

genealogical information a few days earlier asked for further assistance. Laying the missive on the counter, Juanita accompanied the patron to the reference room. As they examined old city directories, Juanita glanced up periodically to see if she was needed in the reading room. Traffic grew heavy after school, but neither assistant signaled for help.

When the woman pronounced herself satisfied, Juanita returned to the checkout desk. Her letter lay on the floor, evidently brushed off by someone. At least it wasn't covered with dirty footprints, she thought wryly, scooping it up and returning to the office to sign it.

Lee Nguyen arrived, looking too delicate to manage her big stack of schoolbooks. She wore a red plaid dress, a yellow sweater and a perky bow in her dark hair. Her eyes shone as she gazed around her.

"Gee, look at all the books. You're lucky to work here."

"I think so too. I always have something to read."

"Maybe I'll be a librarian. If I don't become a doctor or an astronaut."

Confident Lee would be whatever she decided to be, Juanita led her to the office and got her a soft drink from the refrigerator. She laid pencils handy, while Lee removed her sweater and climbed onto a chair at the worktable. Mavis poked her head in the door.

"Some boy's out here to see you."

"Tell him to come on in."

Eddie entered the office, pale, hesitant and clearly wishing himself somewhere else. Juanita made introductions, motioned Eddie to a chair beside Lee and handed him a drink.

"Lee," she said, "Eddie'll want to hear all about how you came to this country, about the boat you left Vietnam in and so on. And be sure to spell names of people and places, very slowly so he can write them down."

An old hand at telling her story to non-Vietnamese

audiences, Lee nodded longsufferingly at the insult to her intelligence. But Juanita couldn't explain her instructions were really for Eddie's benefit, as reassurance he could handle this. The subject began to talk about herself, the nervous interviewer watching her open-mouthed.

"My name's really Lien, L-I-E-N." She paused while he laboriously printed the letters in a notebook. "I go by Lee because it's easier for Americans. My family name is spelled N-g-u-y-e-n, pronounced 'win' like in 'win the game.' We put the family name first in Vietnamese, not last like you do in English."

A flush on Eddie's thin cheeks betrayed embarrassment, but he gamely kept writing. Juanita left, saying, "I'll be at the desk if you need me."

Seated at the circulation desk, she kept an ear cocked toward the open office door. At first Lee's voice delivered a monologue. Then Eddie's joined in, quavery at first, steadying as he evidently realized he wasn't dealing with *Bruce* Lee in drag.

An hour or so later, their talk ceased. Lee came into the reading room carrying books and sweater and smiling as if she had aced an easy exam.

"We're through. I gave him the whole story. Ask me tonight if there's anything else he needs to know." She waved to Juanita and left.

Juanita went to the office. "How'd it go?"

"Okay," Eddie said dazedly. "I think, okay."

She glanced over his notes, mostly partial sentences, and queried him to see if he had understood all he had heard. He responded haltingly at first, eyes glued to notebook. But as Juanita nodded at familiar information, he appeared to gain confidence. A respectful note entered his voice as he told how the Nguyen family had sneaked away by boat at night, escaped capture by pirates, spied land after days at sea and endured many months in a crowded Malaysian refugee camp before being allowed to join Bach's sister in the States.

"That's terrific, Eddie," she said when he had finished. "Excellent interview. You've a very good grasp of the material."

The teen's slender face lit with pleasure. He promised to write the paper that night and show it to Juanita tomorrow. She wondered if he really would, or would find an excuse not to once his initial enthusiasm faded. But he swaggered as he left, a fact she chose to take as a good sign.

Near closing time, Meador and Juanita were at the check-out counter when Doug Darrow came in and handed a green sweater to Meador. "Thought you might need this."

Meador blushed. "Thanks. But you didn't need to bother. You could've brought it to Books tonight."

"No trouble. I had these to drop off anyway." Doug laid two large volumes on the counter and turned to leave.

"Wait a sec, Doug," Juanita said. "We got in a book I think you'll like. You can't check it out yet because it's not catalogued, but it's your sort of thing."

He followed her to the office, where she closed the door and handed him a biography of a Civil War general. "This isn't really why I brought you back here, though."

He pressed a palm to his cheek in mock delight. "At last, Juanita, my love. I knew you'd felt it too—this overpowering attraction between us."

"This is serious, Doug. There's an ugly rumor going around that could cost you your job." She told him what Estelle had heard at the beauty shop, confirmed later by her husband.

Doug guffawed. "Juanita, you know what small towns are like. Everybody wants to get something on a schoolteacher."

"Don't be offhand about this, Doug," she said irritably. "School boards have no sense of humor when it comes to something like a teacher selling drugs to kids."

He sobered. "Thanks for telling me, Juanita, but there's an innocent explanation for the guys being at my place. I can give it if I ever have to."

Reassured, Juanita said, "Something else while we're talking just between us, Doug. You and Meador seem to have become friends. Have you noticed a change in him lately? Today— well, look at the quotes he's put up." She explained about the Quote War.

Doug laughed again. "Don't worry, Juanita. Meador'll tell you what's going on when he's ready."

"I wonder if I'll live long enough to hear it."

The teacher took that as the joke she had intended. But after he left, Juanita decided that in view of the threatening calls she had been getting, it wasn't all that funny.

Chapter Twenty-four

Eddie sashayed down the library steps, thinking things had turned out surprisingly well today. For one thing, the Chink—Vietnamese—kid had been easier to understand than he had expected. She had talked too fast at times, but Miss Wills had made him go over it right away, which helped him remember even details he hadn't written down. He gulped in cool air. Maybe he could even manage to write the paper. He wasn't good at writing, but he would try his best and Miss Wills would fix it. She was okay.

His Ford started immediately, its motor smooth as custard pie. But something was nagging at him. When Gib had invited him along that evening last week, being with Gib and helping him out had sounded like fun. Heaving trash out a moving car's window might not sound like a big job, but the sack had to strike the porch just right, making enough noise to scare the heck out of anyone around. Gib had said so.

Only now Eddie didn't feel proud of the memory.

He headed south to Main, then east. As he drove through downtown, Tiffany and Willa came flouncing out of the dress shop at Center and Main. Stuck-up, both of them. They weren't his type anyway.

Who was he kidding? If either girl had smiled at him, he would have soared like the space shuttle. Gib liked to talk about all the women who were crazy about him. Eddie would probably never find anyone.

Throwing that garbage had appeared a harmless prank. But after hearing what the Nguyens had already gone through it seemed kind of rotten, maybe even cowardly? Gib wasn't a coward—he didn't take anything off anybody—still . . .

Eddie skirted a car illegally parked in his lane. More and more he felt doubts about people and ideas he had never questioned before. If Gib was wrong about the Nguyens, for instance, what about all the other stuff he had told Eddie? What about G.O.L.?

No, he mustn't doubt Guardians of Liberty.

All the same, Eddie hoped Gib wouldn't ask him along if he did something more to the Nguyens. Lee wasn't a friend of his, but she had guts. Eddie had a feeling that if she knew he had thrown that sack she wouldn't even bother getting mad. She would just shrug her thin shoulders and march scornfully away.

Somehow it seemed important not to earn Lee Nguyen's contempt.

Chapter Twenty-five

At Tuesday evening's Books meeting, Juanita arrived just as the group were positioning themselves for the discussion. She grabbed a cup of decaf and three of Doug's store-bought sugar cookies, and joined the Bromptons at a table. The abstracter smiled distantly, probably embarrassed by his recent revelation. From Eva's easy manner toward both of them, Juanita guessed he had not confessed to his wife.

"This book," Katherine said, holding up a copy of *The Prince* as she sat in prim shirtwaist at the desk, "has been called a handbook for dictators. Is that a fair description of it?"

"Yes," Cyril said. His glasses perched atop his bare crown, giving him the air of a studious Humpty Dumpty. "It says rulers do what they have to to stay in power. And 'That war is just which is necessary,' is another way of saying 'the end justifies the means.'"

"That bothered me," said Eva, roundly pretty in a barn-red slacks set. "There's nothing in it about a ruler trying to do what's right. Morals are just left out of this book."

"Not completely, Eva." Doug lolled in his chair, a picture of repose that Juanita doubted would last given the controversial topic. "Machiavelli says a prince should seem to be kind, but that being good to his subjects doesn't work."

"That's awfully pessimistic." Eva took knitting needles and blue wool from a tote bag and began to knit. "Good people don't *always* appear weak or get taken advantage of."

"Is it fair to say," Katherine prompted, "that heads of government live by a different standard than the rest of us?"

"Of course." Earl Trevethan slapped his book against the table. "Governments have the right to protect themselves. Machiavelli's just saying that rulers have tough choices to make, so they should bite the bullet and make them." He cut his dark eyes at Doug. "Try too hard to avoid war, like Chamberlain, and you get war anyway. A worse one."

Doug jerked forward, jostling Roy Boston's elbow. "I'm sick of that example being used to justify any conflict anybody wants to get into."

"Truth hurts, doesn't it, Darrow?"

"*Truth* doesn't. But you wouldn't recognize truth, Trevethan."

"Putting aside the morality issue a moment," Katherine hurriedly said, "what do you think of Machiavelli as a tactician, and an observer of world politics?"

"Pretty astute," said Cyril. "He gives specific examples of what has worked and what hasn't."

"Seems like a sharp strategist," Meador agreed.

"He's right about a ruler needing to take sides when neighboring countries fight," Trevethan said. "Nobody likes a fence-sitter."

"Sure of that, Earl?" said Boston, rubbing away at his chin. "If two neighbors were battling over a property line and you supported one, that could make the other your enemy."

"Speaking of fence-sitting," Pugh said, smiling slyly at Boston, "I understand some in Wyndham won't openly support either commission candidate just in case the other wins." He turned and winked at Juanita.

The lawyer thoughtfully thumbed through his copy of *The Prince*.

"Interesting point, Mr. Pugh," Katherine said. "Machiavelli is advising a head of state. Does his advice apply to local government officials as well?"

Debate of the point became high-spirited. Boston was uncharacteristically silent, one hand kneading his chin. Juanita saw a sleuthing opportunity.

"I wonder about one point," she put in. "Machiavelli says rulers should encourage opposition to themselves so they can look powerful crushing it. Do you suppose world leaders sometimes do manufacture wars they're sure they can win easily?"

"Don't be naive, Wills," Trevethan growled. "Sure they do."

"Maybe even local politicians manipulate us."

Katherine raised an eyebrow. "Are you suggesting, Miss Wills, that office-seekers sometimes fund opposing candidates so when they win it seems a greater triumph?"

"Could be." Juanita felt adrenalin flowing. Her voice grew louder. "Or a candidate could put out outlandish charges against himself—too wild to be believed—and get his opponent blamed for playing dirty politics. The sympathy vote might let him win."

Cyril appeared unconcerned, Boston engrossed in his book, Pugh thoughtful.

"A good point, Miss Wills," the banker mused. "I bet that's exactly what's happened."

"Too devious," said Eva, shaking her head.

"*Or*," said Juanita, finding the game heady, "if a proposal came before City Council, whoever led the fight for it might encourage token opposition to make himself look good."

She noticed beads of perspiration now glittered on Boston's forehead.

"You mean," Doug said with a wicked grin in the attorney's direction, "some lawyer could justify charging a higher fee that way?"

Boston raised his head finally, eying Doug acidly.

Juanita turned to Katherine. "Machiavelli might've known about political strategy, but not about other things." She found a place in her copy and read: "'. . . fortune is a woman, and if you wish to keep her under it is necessary to beat and ill-use her . . .'" Juanita tossed the book on the table. "He hadn't a clue about women."

"Sounds accurate to me, *Ms.* Wills." Trevethan wore a

superior smirk.

"At least Machiavelli had the excuse of living 500 years ago, Earl."

Doug led the general laughter.

"Maybe that's why Earl's not married?" Eva said sweetly. "He can't find a woman who enjoys being beaten?"

Several men groaned.

"Cold, Eva," Doug said. "I bet you actually like it when Cyril chases you around the bedroom with a whip."

Eva smiled kittenishly. Her husband avoided her eyes.

At home later, Juanita made hot chocolate, got pad and pen and sat in robe and slippers at her kitchen table, trying to organize what she had learned relating to Asher's death. She headed pages with names of individuals and made two columns on each, titled "Militia" and "Zoning." Superficially the two lines of inquiry didn't seem to meet, but she couldn't yet rule out a connection. She had hoped being at Books tonight might jog her memory about whatever clue had tried to surface last week, but it hadn't.

Juanita began with Katherine. Though she couldn't believe the elderly woman was involved in criminal activity, Katherine had behaved oddly when asked if she knew of a hate group in the area. She was also a cryptogram fan, and there was that cipher found in Boston's book.

As Juanita recalled the decoded message, one detail came back to her. The meeting at "the farm" was to be Tuesday at 10:00 p.m.

This was Tuesday. And it was nearly 9:30. Perhaps the place she had followed Eddie to last night was that very farm.

Hastily throwing on jeans and sweatshirt, Juanita dashed to her Chevy, which fortunately started after only two tries. She exceeded the speed limit going west from Wyndham and precisely at 9:55 reached the place where Eddie had turned off the highway.

Tonight, seeing a tranquil moonlit scene and a shut gate, she drove past, turned and parked on the opposite shoulder some yards away, her car partly obscured by overhanging branches. Cutting the motor, she watched for signs of activity. Though she waited almost an hour, with autos and trucks whizzing past in both directions, no one turned into the gravel road nor came down it.

At last she started home, thinking that the farm must be somewhere else or the "special unit" had already congregated and closed the gate before she arrived. Or the message was an old one, referring to some previous Tuesday. Or the cipher had absolutely nothing to do with whatever Eddie and Jeffcoat had been doing last evening.

As Juanita passed Doug's house on her way back to town, she remembered he called his place "the farm." She slowed and crawled past, but all looked quiet tonight. Doug's old Jeep sat under the yard light, the only vehicle in sight.

When she got home again, she decided she was too tired to finish sorting clues and stuffed the papers in her bag to work on at the library. Maybe she would inform Wayne about that bookmark, also mention the hate literature at Fuller's home and the campaign poster in Trevethan's workshop. If all that went well, perhaps—just perhaps—she would tell him about trailing Eddie.

It would be a tricky interview, however. Wayne would interpret her activities as barging into his case again. Of course that might not matter too much if her information helped solve the Asher matter.

"Right, Juanita," she muttered aloud. "And buggy whips and treadle sewing machines will become hot items at Wal-Mart."

Chapter Twenty-six

By Wednesday morning Juanita had definitely decided to talk to Wayne. She looked forward to seeing him, but dreaded his reaction. Maybe if she had her facts well organized, she could convince him her snooping had been worthwhile. Seated in the library office, coffee and Danish at her elbow, she jotted information on the "suspect" pages she had begun last night. When she finished, she leaned back to study Katherine's sheet.

Nothing on the "Zoning" side. Under "Militia," there was only the elderly woman's liking for cryptograms—which proved nothing—and her reaction when asked if she knew of militia activity. Wayne would hoot at such "evidence," assuming he listened to Juanita at all. She drew a large "X" across the Books moderator's page.

Earl Trevethan's looked more promising, containing notes in both columns. Under "Zoning," there was his enmity toward Asher, under "Militia" his right-wing militarism, his dislike of Asians and the fact that a light car—possibly his gray one—had been used in harassing the Nguyens. Perhaps most damaging, Vivian had connected him to Gib Cooper, the one person whose guilt Juanita felt sure of. She put a check beside Trevethan's name, marking him as a definite suspect.

Restless, Juanita rose and strode about the office, pausing at the window to gaze out on the sunshiny day. In a backyard lawn overlooked by the office, green had largely crowded out tan—mowing season couldn't be far off. Two small boys in sweaters and corduroy pants tossed a baseball.

She returned to her desk and Roy Boston's page. Under "Zoning," she had Asher's opposition to the shopping center. Also, the minister might have threatened to expose the lawyer for bribery. Boston appeared to have an unbreakable alibi for the time of the church incident, but could have hired men to scare the preacher. The two lines of detection might even come together here. If the attorney were part of a paramilitary organization, he might have convinced other members to attack the minister as his revenge over the zoning battle.

Then there was that trashy campaign poster, smacking of the same mean spirit as in the Asher attack and the threats of the Nguyens. Boston seemed to be somehow involved in the Piersall-Shipman race. Juanita wondered if he had had a hand in the handbill's production.

Also that cipher, with its suggestion of paramilitary activity, pointed to the lawyer, though his denial about it had seemed sincere. Perhaps someone was trying to frame him as revenge over the zoning matter? Juanita dismissed that idea as wildly improbable. Besides, to be an effective frame-up the coded note ought to contain clear evidence of criminal activity. It didn't.

Chewing prune Danish, Juanita decided the many "if's" about Boston warranted a check by his name.

Next came Cyril Brompton. She had nothing under "Zoning" and little under "Militia." The ski mask clue had so far come to naught. And Cyril had explained the post office box she had half suspected of being a militia mail drop. As for his ability to slip in and out of downtown offices, possibly allowing him access to Boston's library book, that definitely seemed to be reaching. With relief, she drew an "X" across his sheet.

The telephone rang, and she answered. "Stickler Simon" Simms, fussbudget accountant, spoke grumpily into her ear.

"We have to cancel tomorrow's library oversight-committee meeting to go over your report. Two members have the flu. I'll phone later to re-schedule."

"No problem." She could manage to exist quite a while without seeing Simon's dour face.

Juanita reached Willard Pugh's page. Regarding "Zoning" she had nothing, save that his support of Asher had proved to cover a hidden agenda. She wondered if his support of Shipman for commissioner was any more disinterested. On the "Militia" side, some of his comments at Books suggested sympathy for such groups, though these might be his queer way of teasing. Too, his bank had once owned Jeffcoat's farm, where such an organization might be meeting. It didn't own it now, though, and according to the papers in the court clerk's office Federal National hadn't profited from the foreclosure beyond collecting the amount owed on its mortgage.

That connection to the mysterious property bothered her, however. She drew a question mark by Pugh's name.

She studied Doug Darrow's sheet, as reluctant to suspect him as Cyril. But regarding the "Militia" inquiry, Doug's vehement anti-war stance could be elaborate camouflage for his involvement with such an organization. A popular teacher, he was in a position to attract high school boys to a cause. Perhaps Asher had even known of such recruiting locally and threatened to expose the fact. Reluctantly, she put a check by Doug's name.

Doubting people she liked was getting to her, and the worst was yet to come. Slipping the papers into her handbag, Juanita went to the circulation desk and said to her assistants, "How's it going?"

"How's *what* going?" Mavis replied darkly. "Shouldn't you ask *where* something's going, not how?"

Juanita stifled a nasty retort. She put up with Mavis and paid her salary, she didn't owe her original conversation too. She indulged briefly in her favorite daydream, today favoring the anthill-honey torture for Mavis, an oldie but a goody.

"We've had a lot of people in," Meador said. "Your buddy the genealogy lady asked for you. I said you were busy and I couldn't disturb you. She found what she needed herself."

"Thanks."

When Juanita returned to the office, she had to consider Meador himself. Under "Zoning" she had nothing, but "Militia" proved more worrisome, especially in view of his militaristic quotes lately. A paramilitary group just might appeal to his need to feel powerful. On Monday night he must have gone either to that mysterious farm or to Doug's place, probably the latter since Doug had returned his sweater to him Tuesday. Why had Meador appeared embarrassed about it?

Her young colleague's size made him a possibility for Paunchy Guy, though she couldn't see him asserting control over Cooper as P.G. had over A.G. In fact, Juanita couldn't believe Meador would get involved in something like the church incident. But she put a question mark on his page.

She had also prepared sheets for Shem Jeffcoat and Walt Fuller, with notations for both on the "Militia" side. Jeffcoat had ties to that suspicious property, was the right size for Teeny Guy and had behaved oddly at Asher's funeral. Cheerfully, Juanita put a check mark by his name.

Another thought occurred. If Jeffcoat's land was the mysterious "farm," Doug's must be in the clear. So even if Meador had gone to Darrow's Monday, both he and Doug must be innocent.

Except the militia could have more than one meeting place.

Juanita stood and pedaled her arms, working out tension. She thought about Walt Fuller, his inquiry after Asher at the hospital and the right-wing materials on his bookshelves.

Oh! She dropped her arms as she recalled something. The phrase "guardians of liberty" had occurred often in the one book she had looked at.

Guardians of Liberty? G.O.L.?

That clinched matters. Wayne surely couldn't dismiss *all* the suspicious occurrences. Juanita checked her watch. Late morning. She had been working on the lists quite a while. She decided to try to catch him at the police station rather than calling first.

Luck was with her. As she entered the station foyer, Wayne stood at a vending machine, grimacing as he drank from a paper cup. At first, his eyes lit with pleasure. Then evidently remembering he was mad at her, he adopted a coolly indifferent expression.

"Hello, Juanita. What brings you here?"

"Can we talk somewhere private, Wayne? It's important."

He hesitated. "I suppose." He ushered her down a corridor to an interview room and shut the door behind them. Motioning her to a seat, he sat across the table watching her warily, like a toddler expecting a scolding for something he didn't recall doing. She itched to ruffle his hair, but restrained herself.

"Wayne, I know you told me to stay out of the Asher case, but . . ."—at his fierce look, she hurried on before he could throw her out—"I've found out some things you need to know."

His lips tightened, but he said nothing.

She laid the cipher and her translation on his desk. Wayne eyed her impassively as she told of finding the bookmark, omitting only her suspicion that Boston had tried to pass it to Meador. When she mentioned following Eddie, Wayne opened his mouth to speak, but Juanita forestalled him.

"I'd bet Eddie was going to a militia meeting, Wayne, the same bunch responsible for Asher's death."

She told about seeing Shem Jeffcoat enter the suspect land just after Eddie and of uncovering Jeffcoat's link to it at the courthouse. Wayne jotted notes on a pad of paper. When Juanita paused for a long breath, he looked up at her, his face a study.

"Even if you think I had no business doing what I did, Wayne," she continued, "I really wish you'd go check out that farm. Something peculiar's going on there."

"Juanita," he said at last, with less hostility than she had expected, "even if there is such an outfit operating there, it's outside the city limits. I don't have jurisdiction. I'd have to involve the county sheriff, and you haven't given me enough probable cause. Eddie and Jeffcoat could just have been going hunting, with the owner's permission."

Encouraged by his reasonable tone, she told Wayne about the other trail she had been following, the zoning controversy. "You said yourself someone might be trying to make you suspect a Klan-type group. I think it's possible Asher made lasting enemies during the shopping-center battle, and they trashed his church as revenge."

Wayne's silence lasted a full minute this time, as if he were considering how much to say.

"We've looked into that, Juanita," he said finally. "So far that possibility seems less promising than the militia one." His voice held only a hint of sarcasm as he added, "I gather you think so too, since you took the extraordinary step of following Eddie."

He peered at the cipher on the desk in front of him. "Special unit. The major. I suppose you've handled this so much there's no hope of prints."

"'Fraid so. I'd no reason at first to think it was a clue."

"Leave it with me. We'll give it the once-over anyway. Be sure to let Sara fingerprint you on your way out. Or do we already have you on file?"

"Why would you? This is my first brush with the police—unless you count all those times on your couch, and mine. Another thing, Wayne." She told about returning to the former Jeffcoat farm last night and of finding the gate shut.

He looked irritated, but the emotion was quickly replaced by another, something like fear. For her? Recalling how she had resented her young husband's risk-taking, Juanita shifted uncomfortably in her chair.

Wayne shook his head sadly. "Juanita, Juanita."

Partly as a distraction, she mentioned Fuller's books and the recurring phrase she had noticed in one. "So maybe 'G.O.L.' stands for Guardians of Liberty, the name of a super-patriot group."

Wayne's eyes widened. "You know, you might actually have something there."

"And, Wayne, this could be unrelated, but—." She told about the Nguyens' problem, while he made more notes. "My neighbors weren't going to tell you, but I thought you ought to know."

"Glad you told me." Wayne waited briefly. "That it?"

She nodded.

"Thanks for bringing these things to my attention, Juanita. I'll look into the areas that seem fruitful."

So he was retreating into formality, she thought with annoyance. But at least he had heard her out. They sat quietly, neither looking at the other. Juanita considered revealing the anonymous phone calls, to prolong the time with him. But the caller had ordered her off the case, and Wayne would do the same. She rose to leave.

"Just a second, Juanita," he said, rising too. "You've turned up a fact or two that may help. But now you've got to butt out and leave the investigation entirely to me. I want your word you will quit 'sleuthing.'"

She eyed him without comment.

"This could be dangerous, Juanita. A man's been beaten to death already. And if right-wing fanatics are out there with weapons, someone else could get killed before it's over.

"That could be—you."

The anxiety in his voice brought tears to her own eyes. Assent rose to her lips, but she swallowed it.

"I don't think I can promise that, Wayne. This involves

friends of mine."

His lips compressed again, and she expected a tongue-lashing. His soft reply surprised her.

"It concerns people I care about too. I hope we don't both regret your stubbornness later."

Juanita left the station with tears streaming down her cheeks. It had been good to talk to Wayne, even officially, a relief to share many of her worries. But reconciliation between them did not seem imminent.

She just couldn't do as he had asked. Not only did the image of Asher's bloody head remain in her mind, not only did the bullying of innocents offend her sense of fair play, but she resented being forced to suspect people she liked and had trusted. Confident as she felt of Wayne's detective skills, the case had become her personal crusade.

Juanita hoped once it was solved she and Wayne could return to the easy, loving relationship they had had. But she feared something had already fundamentally changed.

Chapter Twenty-seven

Before Juanita returned to the library, she stopped by the computer place for floppy-disk mailers and manila envelopes. She could have sent Meador, but balked at letting fear of Gib Cooper control her actions. Besides, she wanted to see him now that his beating victim had died. She didn't expect he would look ravaged by guilt, but one never knew.

She entered the store, gathered her items and approached the counter, where two other customers stood already. Acting the part of unhurried shopper, she put her selections on the counter and meandered toward the repair shop, pausing near its doorway to think of a plausible question to ask about her hard drive.

Cooper came out of the shop carrying a PC, his eyes on the monitor atop it. He passed Juanita, set the computer on the counter and spoke to the clerk. When he turned back toward the shop, he found Juanita in his path. She felt a panicky impulse to dash from the store, but refused to give him the satisfaction. She stood her ground, forcing herself to meet his gaze without flinching.

If knowing he had helped cause Asher's death bothered the repairman, he hid it well. The hard gray eyes bored into hers. A muscle in his cheek twitched.

Years of staring contests as a child stood her in good stead. He blinked first, and the tiny victory cheered her. She hoped he hadn't noticed her hands shaking.

That afternoon Meador showed a hesitant Eddie into the library office. Neither young man gave any sign of knowing each other from militia meetings. Eddie appeared tired and anxious.

"Got the paper," he mumbled. He dropped a notebook on the desk, opened it and removed two sheets of paper.

Juanita took them. Neatness didn't appear to be Eddie's long suit. Smudged printing, crossings-out, insertions and idiosyncratic spelling made some portions almost indecipherable. His "E's" were, as usual, backwards. Punctuation and grammar needed considerable aid, and she made him use a dictionary to correct spellings. His sentences tended to the short and choppy, so Juanita helped him combine some using conjunctions and dependent clauses.

But the effort proved better than she had expected, with surprisingly good organization and a respectful, even admiring tone toward Lee and her family's experiences. Eddie made the changes suggested and at Juanita's insistence recopied the paper. Finally he handed her the clean copy, watching tensely as she read it.

"This is a really good paper, Eddie," she said when she had finished. "I'm proud of you."

His taut body relaxed, and he appeared to grin all over. "Really? You think it's okay?"

"Absolutely. I know you worked hard on it. You did an excellent job."

The compliment produced an unaccustomed glow on his cheeks. Juanita suspected Eddie had received precious little praise in his life.

His face fell. "Ol' Lady Hawkins won't believe I wrote it. I never done nothing good before."

"Be honest with her, Eddie. Tell her I read it over and helped you revise sentence structure and correct grammar and spelling. But stress the fact that you did the interview and actually wrote the paper yourself—show her the notes you took and this rough draft." Juanita smiled reassuringly. "She can call and ask me about it if she wants. I'll back you up."

That eased his worries. Wreathed in smiles, he collected his books to leave.

"Thanks, Miss Wills, thanks a whole lot. If I can ever help you with something, just ask."

"There's only one thing you could do for me, Eddie. And

you already know what that is."

His smile vanished again. He stared at his own hand. "I can't talk about that, Miss Wills. I just can't." He looked up, eyes pleading.

She caved. Whatever was keeping him quiet must be powerful.

"All right, Eddie, but if you ever want to talk . . ."

He nodded, said "Thanks again," and escaped out the door.

Juanita remained at her desk brooding. She felt sure he was mixed up in something illegal, possibly violent. And maybe others she knew were too. Why? For Eddie, the reason might be a simple need to gain the approval of others.

Maybe of one other.

She glanced at her associates in the reading room. Since Meador's show of spunk, Mavis had appeared demoralized, Meador happy as a kid with a new video game. Juanita wondered how long the current state of affairs would last.

When she arrived home that evening and opened the screen door, an envelope that had been tucked inside fell out. She picked it up, saw on the front one word, "Wilz."

She unlocked the door, set her bag on the couch, ripped open the envelope and removed a single sheet of notebook paper. Block letters said, "Stay out of wat don't concern yu. This is yur last warnin." It was unsigned.

Dropping note and envelope, she hurried outside to look for the deliverer. No one in sight up or down the street. She was about to go back in when something beside the porch steps caught her eye. Kneeling, she saw in the low light of early evening what looked like nutshells. She carried a few into the house and examined them under strong lamplight.

The shells were thin and brown, with small surface bumps. Juanita felt as if someone had punched her hard in the stomach.

They were lychee-nut hulls.

Chapter Twenty-eight

Juanita went around the neighborhood asking if anybody had seen someone at her house that day. No one had. Most neighbors worked during the daytime, and even the curious elderly lady across the street had been in Tulsa for medical tests that afternoon.

Having someone actually come to her home seemed worse than hearing that hushed voice on the phone. The lychee husks bothered her too, pointing as they did to either Doug or Meador.

But during the night—another long restless one—Juanita decided it was a bit too convenient that the hulls were lying there in plain sight when she found the note. As if someone had wanted them found. As if he/she had deliberately tried to implicate one man or the other.

Who had done it, though? She doubted Gib Cooper even knew either Doug or Meador—unless they were in a militia together—much less knowing they liked dried lychees. And such a frame-up appeared way too subtle for Cooper.

She considered each name on her suspect sheets. Though she had questions about many people, there was nothing conclusive on anyone. She must be missing some important link among clues that would help her zero in on one individual . . . .

The next morning she placed the warning note and its envelope in a plastic bag, put that in her purse and walked to the library, huddled in a jacket against a nippy wind. When she reached her office she phoned Wayne, but found him out. Later that morning, he returned her call.

"What's up? I've been out working an accident."

She told him about the threatening note, the telephone

calls that preceded it and the reptile in her car. After a brief silence, he spoke with thinly disguised annoyance.

"Why didn't you mention those anonymous calls and the snake yesterday?"

"I—guess I—didn't—take them seriously before."

Another pause, Wayne counting to ten, she guessed. "You got the note at the library? I'll come by and get it, though there probably won't be prints. Try not to worry."

Minutes later he arrived, followed Juanita to the office and closed the door. As they faced each other, his aftershave pleasantly citrusy, she wanted to lean into him, feel his arms encircle her. Instead, she handed him the plastic bag.

"I haven't handled those much. Just when I opened the envelope."

Wayne's face seemed a study of emotions. She guessed he was trying to decide whether to hug her or scold her. The latter impulse won.

"You know, Juanita, this doesn't really surprise me. When amateurs try to play detective, they put themselves and others at risk."

"You think the threats are real, then." In view of his obvious worry, she decided to ignore the lecture.

"We don't dare assume they're not. You could've unwittingly stumbled onto something that frightened Asher's attackers. Describe that snake again."

She did so, letting pass the condescension in "unwittingly stumbled onto something."

"Sounds like a bull snake, all right." His eyes narrowed. "You told me everything now?"

"I think so." Juanita sat at her desk, took the sheaf of minidossiers from her handbag and handed it to him. "But just in case, here's what I know so far about various people. Hope you can make more sense of it all than I did."

Wayne dropped into a chair, glanced through the sheets

and gave a low whistle. "Katherine Greer? You think she's involved?"

Juanita laughed sheepishly. She heard an answering chuckle in his throat before he turned it to a cough.

"Not really. But I was considering all possibilities."

"Wouldn't be surprised to see my own name here." Wayne lowered his voice to a whisper. "Does Meador know you suspect him?"

At her blush, he grinned.

"I'll take these pages if it's okay. By the way, we came up empty for prints on that bookmark—except yours, of course."

Wayne rose and gave her an uncertain look, then approached her chair. Now what? she thought. Another reprimand?

He leaned over and brushed her lips with his, the light touch warming her to her toes. The kiss clearly stirred him too. When he spoke, his voice sounded husky.

"This doesn't appear to be a game, Juanita. Yesterday I asked you, today I'm making it an order: Stay out of the case."

He didn't wait for a reply—fortunately, since he would not have liked it.

But the command was probably unnecessary, she reflected. Unless her letter to the Secretary of State produced useful information, she had run out of ideas. And government agencies being what they were, it could be a long time before a response from that office came.

Thinking about that letter, Juanita recalled she had left it on the circulation desk, then later found it on the floor. Anyone might have read it and learned she was checking on that land's ownership. The warning note had appeared at her house the very next day.

Hunting up Mavis in the stacks, Juanita asked who had come in while she had been helping the genealogy woman Tuesday. The assistant put down a stack of magazines and propped one hand against an angular hip.

"Let's see—we had quite a bit of traffic. Only person I recall for sure was Miss Greer, because she requested a book through inter-library loan. Why?"

"No reason. Just wondering."

To Mavis's evident disappointment, Juanita retreated to the office, where she sat considering this news. She still couldn't see Katherine as a suspect, but the retired teacher might have mentioned the letter's contents to another party, maybe the same one who was already heckling Juanita. . . .

She thought back to that first anonymous call, wondering if she had learned something incriminating just before which might have precipitated it. She didn't think so. The call had come right after the discussion of Thoreau at Books, and she had hardly begun investigating by then.

At least her relationship with Wayne seemed to be undergoing a gradual defrosting. At the rate it was occurring, he might escort her to her retirement party thirty years hence.

Chapter Twenty-nine

After work that evening Juanita ate a quick supper and went to do her WRA shift. As she drove along Cherry Street approaching the charity's office, she met Trevethan's gray sedan. She waved at him, but he stared straight ahead as if preoccupied.

Juanita pulled into the parking lot beside the old warehouse and parked next to the van, the lone vehicle on the lot. She was reaching for the flowerpot to get the building key when the door opened and Estelle Pugh came out.

"Juanita, what are you *doing* here? You *do* remember you agreed to *trade* with me, don't you?" Estelle's tone said if Juanita was going back on their agreement she wouldn't stand for it.

"Darn, I forgot. Where's your Lincoln? I figured no one was here."

"It's acting *up*. A *neighbor* dropped me off earlier. I'll call *Willard* to pick me up when I'm finished."

"Happy collecting, then. Guess I'll go home and read. The library got in a new Marcia Muller."

Typically of late, her Chevy resisted starting. Juanita tried it three times, then waited before trying again. She really must trade as soon as possible, she thought. So far she had lucked out, but probably couldn't much longer.

Estelle closed the building, dropped the key in her bag and crawled into the van. Looking in the rearview mirror, she arranged her hair and checked her makeup. At last the Chevy started, and Juanita slipped it into gear and drove off the lot. She had gone a block or so, anticipating a leisurely evening, when from behind her came an explosion.

BOOM! In that quiet neighborhood, it sounded as if the world was ripping apart.

Juanita jumped an inch off the seat. She stomped the brake, and the car screeched to a stop. In her mirror, she saw the van burning, tongues of red, orange and blue adding to its already wild color scheme.

Estelle! Juanita reversed her auto in a half circle, shifted into drive and raced back to the office. Parking a safe distance from the van, she jumped out and ran toward it.

The blast had ripped off the hood and flung it away somewhere. Flames leapt from the opening. The driver's door hung by one hinge. The top half of Estelle dangled from the front seat. Her silver-gray coiffure had escaped its hair-pins, and several strands brushed the concrete. Her legs seemed to be pinned inside.

Juanita dropped to the ground and crawled to avoid the worst heat and smoke. Nearing the van, she saw that Estelle's eyes were closed and a deep cut slashed her forehead. Soot, glass shards and other debris made a mockery of her carefully applied makeup.

What to do? Juanita wondered. Estelle might already be dead from injuries or smoke inhalation, but maybe not. Juanita crept nearer, reached out to touch her.

Just then a wind gust billowed smoke directly in Juanita's face. Choking, she panicked, sure she was being burnt alive. Blindly, eyes smarting, she hurled herself backward out of the acrid cloud. Skulking away to fresher air, she inhaled in gulps.

She mustn't give up. Screwing her courage for another effort, Juanita took in a huge breath and held it while inching toward the burning vehicle.

She again reached the auto, raised herself, grasped the silk-encased legs and pulled. One leg held fast, pinned—Juanita now saw—by the steering wheel, bent sideways in the blast. Her hand touched searing metal. She flinched.

The heat was intense, seemed to fry her eyelids. A wave of faintness swept over her. She mustn't lose consciousness. Once more, she retreated to safety.

She was beginning a third try when a strong hand grabbed her shoulder.

"You crazy, lady?" said a gruff voice. "That gas tank could blow any second!"

Juanita hadn't heard the man run up behind her, but let him lead her to a low brick wall several yards away. They threw themselves on the ground behind it, dead weeds and gravel digging into Juanita's bare palms, just as another blast ripped the van.

Twisted metal, wires and mangled plastic flew everywhere. Flames engulfed the hull. Through the smoke and fire, Juanita glimpsed Estelle still hanging from the van.

She turned to her rescuer. He appeared sixtyish, with dirt-streaked face and unkempt beard. His tattered jeans jacket, grubby shirt and wrinkled dress pants must not have seen a laundry for weeks, maybe months.

He looked gorgeous to her.

"Thank you," she said, keenly aware of the words' inadequacy. "Where's a phone? I've got to get help for Estelle."

An ambulance screamed up and jerked to a halt. Someone in the area must have called, Juanita realized gratefully. The fire blazed less briskly now. The EMTs managed to get Estelle out and went to work over her.

Two police cars arrived, Wayne in one. He surveyed the scene and spoke with the other officers and ambulance attendants, gravely shaking his head at something one of the latter said. Then he noticed the two faces peering over the wall and walked over to them.

"You folks see what happened here?"

"That van just blew up," the derelict muttered, getting to his feet. "Shook the houses. This lady about got herself wiped out."

Juanita rose. Wayne looked at her for the first time, and she saw his eyes register her identity.

"What you doing here? Wait,"—he scratched the back of his neck—"this is your night to drive the van, isn't it?"

His head swiveled toward the smoldering van and the victim's limp form. His stricken eyes returned to Juanita just as her own mind grasped a chilling fact.

The explosion had been meant for her.

Chapter Thirty

A nearby street lamp came on, lighting the three of them as they sat on the low wall. As Wayne took a statement from the man, Elzie Mattox, Juanita noticed his hand shaking. A vein pulsed in his wide forehead. Finally Wayne thanked the man and said he could go. Juanita asked Mattox if she could reward him in some way, but he waved away her gratitude and sauntered off.

"Who knew you were changing shifts with Estelle tonight?" Wayne asked in a voice not quite steady.

He looked especially appealing with the dying flames dancing in his eyes, Juanita thought. Their quarrel now seemed unbelievably trivial.

"I don't think I mentioned it to anyone. In fact, I had forgotten myself. I don't know who all Estelle might've told. But she wasn't happy about having to switch, and usually half of Wyndham knew when Estelle Pugh had a grievance." Realizing the woman she was discussing so ungraciously was now dead, Juanita fell silent.

Wayne asked other questions, appearing to grow more agitated as they talked. Finally, he got up and pulled Juanita to her feet.

"I need to ask you something. Over here." He led her around the end of the WRA building, where three tall firs created a dark semi-enclosure, a natural privacy screen. His brawny arms enfolded her, pulling her hard against him. Their mouths found each other, kissing tentatively at first, then eagerly. She caught back a sob of joy.

"That was almost you out there," he said hoarsely. He held her close and with the backs of two fingers gently stroked her cheek. "I've been worried about you, babe, but even I didn't expect this."

Shuddering, she squeezed his hand, unable to speak.

"From now on, you take no more chances. Hear me?"

She nodded numbly, thinking that even eating fresh fruit was taking a chance these days.

"Wish I could stay with you tonight, babe," Wayne went on, "but I'm on duty. When you get home, lock up tight. I'll make sure a patrol car comes by your place often."

His obvious anxiety stiffened Juanita's own backbone. She recovered her power of speech. "I'll be fine, Wayne. Whoever did it surely won't try anything else tonight. And I refuse to live a prisoner of fear."

Wishing she felt as confident as the words sounded, she crawled into the Chevy, which as if to lull her into keeping it started immediately, and drove home. Shaky but in control, she locked the car in the garage and secured doors and windows, shooting home the dead-bolt with special satisfaction.

She hadn't been home long when a tap sounded at the back door. Hurrying to the kitchen, she called, "Bach, is that you?"

"Yes, me. You have time tonight?"

Juanita undid the door and smilingly invited her neighbor in. As she refastened the lock, a departure from her usual practice, Bach looked a question at her.

"I'm being more careful since the preacher got killed and someone threw that stuff at your house," Juanita explained. "How are you and your family doing?"

"Okay."

They sat at the table. Juanita offered hot chocolate, but Bach declined.

"Have you gotten any more letters?"

"No, but Tinh keep gun loaded all time. When he hear car go slow, he get gun. But nobody throw anything more."

"That's good, at least. By the way, Lee was a big help to Eddie. He's grateful, and so am I."

Bach smiled and nodded. They talked of mundane matters,

and when Bach left, Juanita was feeling better.

The ten o'clock news carried a report on the van explosion, noting that Federal authorities—specifically the Bureau of Alcohol, Tobacco and Firearms—would be investigating.

Juanita took a hot bath. As tension eased from her body, she wondered when the bomb had been placed in the van. Except for Saturdays and Sundays, the vehicle was used each evening for collections, seldom at other times because WRA workers found it too conspicuous for errands. Placement must have occurred between Wednesday night's run and this evening. Less than twenty-four hours of opportunity. The best chance had probably been last night, though building and parking lot might have been empty part of today also.

Why it had been placed remained a mystery. If Juanita had learned something that had triggered the attempt on her life, she didn't know what that was.

At least now she wasn't playing a lone hand. The police knew everything she did. But two people had already died, and as Wayne had said, she herself might still be a target. From now on, she would make sure to start her car from a distance using the remote. Bravery didn't have to include stupidity.

Wiring the van unnoticed probably wouldn't have been too hard for the murderer, since it often sat unguarded in a near-deserted section of town. Her own car would pose a greater risk, being mostly in her garage or parked on a well-traveled street near the library.

However, a truly determined person could probably overcome such hindrances.

Chapter Thirty-one

Juanita was preparing to leave for work the next morning, earlier than usual to allow a planned stop, when her doorbell rang. She answered it and found a solemn, stooped man and a smiling, motherly woman standing there. They showed badges and introduced themselves as Russell Mapes and Carolyn Sawyer of the Bureau of Alcohol, Tobacco and Firearms. Sawyer courteously explained that they needed to question Juanita about the previous evening's explosion. She invited them in, put on a pot of coffee and joined them at the kitchen table. The investigators' queries covered much the same territory as Wayne's had last night.

"So you think you were the intended victim, Miss Wills," Mapes said tonelessly, as if being a murder target was nothing out of the ordinary.

Perhaps in his world it wasn't, Juanita thought. "Yes."

"Why do you believe someone would try to kill you?" he went on, as unemotionally as if asking for a cake recipe.

Juanita summarized events of the past two weeks, including the threats she had received and suspicious behavior she had noticed on the part of various Wyndhamites. Mapes watched unblinkingly as she talked. Then Sawyer took her back over it all, asking clarification on some points.

They discussed the security, or lack thereof, at the WRA office. When Juanita mentioned the flowerpot keyholder, Mapes' left eyebrow twitched. She decided that was his way of registering hilarity.

"Can you think of anything else, Miss Wills?" Sawyer said at last. "Anything that might have a bearing on the case?"

"No. I'd say we've covered everything."

They thanked Juanita for her cooperation and told how to reach them if additional details occurred to her. As the two left, Mapes gave Juanita a last mournful look that seemed to say she ought to make a clean breast of things.

She unlocked the garage, went back to the house and started her car with the remote. Gathering a cardigan and a book to return to the library, she got in and drove off. Though her watch said she was now late for work, she decided to pay her planned condolence call on Willard Pugh anyway. Somehow she felt responsible for his wife's death.

When she arrived at Pugh's Tudor-style home, two other vehicles sat in the wide drive, Katherine Greer's yellow Dart and Roy Boston's tan Riviera. They must be here for the same reason she was. Good, she thought, she wouldn't be the only one striving to make conversation.

The housekeeper let Juanita in and led her to a formal parlor with white French provincial furniture and elegant damask drapes. As she entered, Pugh came over and clasped Juanita's hand in both of his.

"Miss Wills," he murmured. "So kind of you to come." His cherubic face sagged, and his blue eyes behind the rimless glasses looked especially watery.

"I'm terribly sorry about Estelle. It was an awful shock." Given the warmth of his greeting, she wished she liked him more.

"I really haven't taken it in yet," he sighed. "When they told me my wife was dead, it was like they were talking about someone else." He studied the wide arch behind Juanita. "I expect her to come walking through that door any moment."

Juanita sat beside Katherine on a silky rose sofa across from Roy Boston, who faced them from a pink love seat. All three said hello in hushed tones. Pugh offered Juanita coffee from a silver urn on the coffee table. Though she was over her limit already, she accepted. Watching him pour, she wondered if Willard and Estelle had loved each other, contrary to appearances. The strain in his face suggested they had.

"You tried to rescue Estelle from that van," he said tremulously, handing Juanita the full cup. "Thank you for that. I'll never forget it." He took a burgundy chair beside Katherine.

"Sorry I couldn't save her, Willard. If it's any comfort, she died quickly."

Katherine eyed Juanita thoughtfully. "Don't you usually drive the van Thursdays, Miss Wills?"

Boston gulped a mouthful of coffee. "That's right—you did last week. So how come Mrs. Pugh was in it last night?"

Juanita explained, the banker nodding as she mentioned the TV spot.

"I made that appointment," he said ruefully. "If I hadn't, Estelle wouldn't have—oh, sorry, Miss Wills, what a thoughtless thing to say."

"It's okay, Willard."

"Then the bomb may have been intended for you, Miss Wills?" Katherine asked.

Deciding the information would probably come out anyway, Juanita said, "I think it was, actually."

Katherine gasped. For several moments, no one spoke.

"Who'd want to kill a librarian?" Boston said, rubbing his chin. "Pretty extreme way to avoid a library fine."

No one laughed at the feeble joke, including the speaker.

"I guess Asher's attackers thought I knew more about them than I had told the police."

"And do you, Miss Wills?" Katherine asked softly.

"If so, I don't know that I know it. I do sometimes feel I'm missing something, though, some clue I can't see the significance of. But that's probably just my overactive imagination."

"Judging by what happened last night, it might be safer not to remember," Boston said. "I'd stay clear of the whole business if I were you."

"Have they any idea yet who placed the bomb, Mr. Pugh?" Katherine asked.

"If so, nobody's told me. Two ATF investigators—a Mrs. Sawyer and a Mr. Mapes—came this morning, but they were fairly noncommittal."

"That pair must start early," Juanita said. "They questioned me today too."

Pugh smiled sadly. "I gathered they're not the only ATF people on the case, but they evidently cover lots of ground. They got me out of bed. I had taken a sleeping pill, knew I'd never rest otherwise. Did they seem surprised to learn the explosion had been meant for you?"

"I doubt anything's surprised Russell Mapes since his first diaper got damp."

"Do be careful, Miss Wills," Pugh said. "We don't want to lose you too."

The others seconded his words.

"I'm probably safe. Now that the Feds are involved, the killer would be crazy to try again."

It wasn't till Juanita was in the car driving away that a sinister interpretation of something Boston had said struck her. "I'd stay clear of the whole business if I were you" sounded a lot like what her anonymous phone caller had been saying.

Chapter Thirty-two

Early that Friday, Mavis struck. Juanita was in the office looking over the mail when her assistant stalked in, face grim, bony body taut with purpose, and ostentatiously hung a strip of paper below the similar ones. Without glancing at her boss, she strode out again. Juanita nearly pulled a muscle getting to the wall to read the new quote.

Generally youth is like the first cogitations,
not so wise as the second.
—Francis Bacon: *Youth and Age*

So it was going to be age versus youth this time. The selection seemed a mild start, but since Mavis had chosen the subject, she must have better stuff in her arsenal for later.

When Meador arrived and saw the note, he gave a grunt of satisfaction and headed to the reference section. Soon he returned with a reply. When he had left, also without comment, Juanita read:

The glory of young men is their strength.
—*Proverbs 20:29*

She yawned. Tame stuff.
Mavis's next offering proved more colorful, however.

Everybody's youth is a dream, a form of
chemical madness.
—F. Scott Fitzgerald: *The Diamond as Big as the Ritz*

Meador retaliated with:

The age is best which is the first,
When youth and blood are warmer.
—Robert Herrick: *Hesperides*

Mavis next offered:

We grow with years more fragile in
body, but morally stouter. . . .
—Logan Pearsall Smith: *Afterthoughts*

Meador answered:

All ills gather together in old age.
—Bion of Borysthenes: in *Diogenes*
Laertius, IV. vii.

Mavis's next sally said:

Age is more just than youth.
—Aeschylus: *Fragments 228*

He responded:

Young men have more virtue than old men;
they have more generous sentiments in
every respect.
—Samuel Johnson: *in Boswell's Life*

Then Mavis began playing hard ball:

Young men think old men are fools;
but old men know young men are fools.
—George Chapman: *All Fools V. i.*

The reply was obvious. Though Meador showed commendable restraint, he finally succumbed and used it:

There is no fool like an old fool.
—John Lyly: *Mother Bombie IV. ii.*

They had been at it thick and fast all morning. Just before noon, Meador was standing beside Juanita's desk telling her about a book he had read on the Battle of Waterloo—his listener wishing he would leave so she could finish a letter—when Mavis walked sedately in. She added a slip to the wall, cut her eyes slyly at Meador and left. It read:

It is impossible to treat quietly
and dispute orderly with a fool.
—Montaigne: *Essays III.viii.*

A shift in topic. How would Meador respond? It wasn't long before Juanita found out.

Wise men have more to learn of fools
than fools of wise men.
—Montaigne: *Essays III. viii.*

In all wars, a pivotal moment occurs. In this one it came shortly after lunch as Meador and Juanita sat in the office eating ice cream cones she had picked up while out doing an errand. Their colleague marched in, head high, shoulders back, wearing a beatific expression, gripping a paper firmly in both hands. Making a ceremony of the act, she taped it below Meador's last slip.

Answer not a fool according to his
folly, lest thou also be like unto him.
—*Proverbs 26:5*

Neither of Mavis's readers then tumbled to the fact that she had just delivered the *coup de grace*.

Meador finished his treat, went to the reference room and brought back three volumes of quotations. While he studied them, Juanita typed an order. Finally he posted a reply:

It is Ill-manners to silence a Fool, and Cruelty to let him go on.
—Benjamin Franklin, *Poor Richard's Almanack*

Juanita considered it an apt response, but no answer came from Mavis. When the three were next in the office together, the older woman read Meador's quote and pointed to her previous one. Meador tried again, returning to the age-youth battle.

The denunciation of the young is a necessary part of the hygiene of older people, and greatly assists the circulation of their blood.
—Logan Pearsall Smith: *Afterthoughts*

Even this failed to move Mavis. She again gestured at the quote she had posted earlier.

Finally the light dawned on both Meador and Juanita. Mavis had suckered him in with the age quotes, knowing he couldn't resist using the "no fool like an old fool" one. That had set him up for the one in which she rejected further participation.

For the time being at least, the Quote War had ended.

Juanita had to admit she would miss it. As for Meador, he showed signs of shock. Mavis had read him well—he had enjoyed their sparring more than he had realized. By using the Quote War itself as her weapon, Mavis had won it.

When that climactic moment occurred in early afternoon, Juanita expected the rest of Friday to be dull. She was wrong. About three-thirty, Meador poked his head in the office and handed her a sealed letter.

"This was lying on the floor by the front door. Don't know how long it's been there."

As he watched with obvious curiosity, she studied the envelope's front. On it, "Mis Wils" had been printed in an awkward schoolboy hand.

"I'll read it later," she said, tossing the missive onto a file cabinet and returning to the publisher's invoice she was checking. A disappointed-looking Meador left.

Juanita finished with the invoice and opened the envelope. The folded piece of notebook paper she took out read:

Need to tauk to you. Now. Cum to the farm.
You no, wher you folod me too. Cum now. Hury.
  —Eddie

The "E's" were all backwards, the spelling of "hury" like that in the boy's rough draft of his paper.

But why meet at "the farm"? Why hadn't Eddie simply talked to her here at the library? Was there something out there he wanted to show her? Eddie had given no sign earlier that he knew she had followed him Monday. Had he only just found out? How?

The note sounded urgent, and might have lain there a while before Meador noticed it. Grabbing her bag, Juanita absentmindedly flipped off the office light.

"In case I'm not back by closing time," she told Mavis, hurrying past the circulation desk, "go ahead and lock up."

Mavis nodded, but her lifted eyebrow said a real librarian wouldn't cut out early on a Friday afternoon.

As Juanita opened the door, a chilly wind greeted her. She

went back for her sweater. Finding the office dark, she felt along the door facing for the switch. A memory fluttered about the edges of her brain, teasing her, the same detail she had been trying to recall since that night at Books.

But like an elusive butterfly the recollection darted away before she could catch it. She had almost gotten it this time.

Chapter Thirty-three

Juanita slowly pulled on her cardigan, struck by a sudden suspicion. What if that note wasn't really from Eddie? What if someone knew of her affection for the boy and was using that against her? She would be taking a risk going to that isolated farm, especially since her old Chevy might not start when she needed it to.

She should let Wayne know. Maybe he would go with her, or would follow her out there. Dropping her handbag on the desk, Juanita shut the door against possible interruption and telephoned the police station. The dispatcher said Wayne had taken the afternoon off to go hunting, and she wasn't expecting him back today.

That seemed odd, Juanita thought, after his complaints about the department being short-handed. The flu situation must have eased. He did deserve a break after all the extra hours he had been putting in. She left a message with the dispatcher in case he should call in.

"Tell him Juanita's gone out to *the farm*. He'll know where."

She then dialed Wayne's home number. No answer.

What to do? On the one hand, the thought of entering that eerie farm frightened her, particularly after one attempt on her life already. And there was no denying the car might fail her.

On the other hand, it hadn't often done so. It usually started after a few tries. Too, the presence of ATF investigators made it unlikely that whoever had planted that bomb would try again. Most importantly, the note appeared to be genuine. A vision of Eddie in desperate trouble, with only her to help him, crowded other thoughts from Juanita's mind. She collected her bag and left again.

Pausing on the library steps, she pressed the button on the

remote. Actually the Chevy had been fairly cooperative since she had begun efforts to replace it, like a recalcitrant child finally convinced of the need to behave. In a way, she would regret letting it go. It started immediately this time, increasing the feeling.

Juanita drove south to Main Street, turning east rather than west as she thought of another possibility. It wouldn't take long to drive by the service station to see if Eddie's blue Fairlane was there. If so, maybe she could convince him to talk somewhere in town, save that drive to the country.

But when she reached the station, not only was the teenager's car not in evidence, neither was Bud's old brown pickup. The only vehicle she saw was a white sedan inside the mechanic's bay. The toes of work boots—Bud's, she assumed—protruded from beneath it.

For good measure Juanita swung by the Wagoner home, circling several blocks before remembering its exact location. All the while, a voice in her head urged haste—if Eddie were in real trouble, delay might be costly.

The Ford wasn't at his home either.

Reluctantly Juanita headed west out of town, urging the Chevy up to the speed limit. What would Eddie have to tell her? The identity of Asher's attackers? That of Estelle's murderer? Something about a militia and its membership?

Busy with her thoughts, she barely saw new-plowed fields and pastures of tender grass she passed. Farmhouses with outbuildings, windbreaks of trees and brush, a lonely convenience store—all flew by her unheeding gaze. She did rouse as she passed Doug's place, but his old two-story with its wide porch and hovering cottonwoods looked serene, with no vehicles in sight. So did the Shipman driveway.

Juanita reached the steel gate, wide open now, slowed and turned in, bouncing through the portal and rumbling across bars of a cattle guard. She half expected an outraged farmer with a shotgun to draw a bead on her from the brush border-ing the creek, but saw no one. Regaining speed, she watched a spume of gravel dust rise in her mirror.

Two hundred yards along the road, she entered a dense stand of trees. Oaks and pecans stood bare-limbed, but full foliage of live oak, magnolia and pine shut out the sun. The trees seemed to press in on her, the atmosphere felt close and airless. Every nerve ending in her body stood at attention. Her eyes darted from road to forest and back. Would armed men step in front of her car and command her to halt? Would Eddie suddenly appear like a wood elf?

Her apprehension increasing, Juanita switched on her headlights. And as the surrounding terrain grew clearer, so did her thought processes. She realized what she had tried to recall after Books, then at the library today, the something that one Books member had known about the church incident that hadn't been in the newspaper. She drove automatically, brain whirling with possibilities. One idea seemed incredible, yet if true it would explain the puzzling and contradictory array of clues she had found. It would mean she had been looking at the case wrong almost from the start.

If it were accurate, she had been used.

Finally the way ahead lightened and the car emerged in a clearing. High branches still hid the sky except for the occa-sional azure patch, but trees had been thinned and lower limbs cut off to allow a settlement of sorts. Ahead sat a small frame house, its right side hidden by close-growing brush. Behind it, barely visible through the trees, were a barn and a large metal Quonset hut. To the dwelling's left lay an unpaved parking lot and a long narrow stretch of terrain dotted with stumps, bri-ars and barbed wire. To Juanita's right, in front of the house, a crude arena appeared.

She slowed her car, switched off the headlights and pulled into the nearly empty parking lot, heavily marked with ruts and tire treads. Eddie's blue Fairlane snuggled against the residence's siding, its hood ornament disappearing into a bush. Juanita parked to the Ford's left, cut her motor, got out and looked around.

The only sound was the hum of a distant automobile engine somewhere. Even birds and squirrels were keeping a low profile. Not a hint of breeze rustled the wealth of foliage around her.

Eddie must be waiting for her inside the house. Juanita circled his car and headed for the little porch. A clumsy walkway of rocks and warped two-by-twelves led to it, but she walked on dead grass to avoid hearing her heels clomp on the boards. Not that being quiet now made any sense—the Chevy's cluttering motor had already announced her arrival.

Was this indeed the meeting place of a militia? What was she getting into? Now she was actually here, Juanita felt her heart pounding. Suppose someone other than Eddie arrived unexpectedly and found her poking about where she didn't belong?

She forced herself to climb the steps. But at the front door her knees buckled. She leaned against the frame, taking deep breaths, wishing she had a gun and knew how to use it. Even more, she yearned to have Wayne here.

Then Juanita thought about Eddie, a good kid, possibly enmeshed in something he didn't fully understand. Maybe he had angered someone powerful in the organization, had endangered his own life. Now he had turned to her. The thought of Eddie in peril, needing her, steadied Juanita.

Deciding not to knock, she turned the doorknob, entered and found herself in a dingy hallway. The smell of dust hung in the air, mingled with some oily odor.

Where could Eddie be? She tried the knob of a door, found it locked. The opposing door didn't open either. She walked down the narrow hallway, several creaking floorboards signaling her progress to anyone listening. At the end of the short hall, she came to two more facing doors.

Still time to back out, she thought. But she had come this far. Taking another deep breath, she twisted the knob of the door on her right. Nothing.

Juanita tried the left one. It opened. She stepped inside.

She still didn't see Eddie. But seated at a grubby desk, child-like in a roomy windbreaker, sat Willard Pugh. The gun in his hand pointed at her.

He was smiling.

Chapter Thirty-four

Dad's old pickup steered like a tank, Eddie thought as he turned onto Main. He hoped none of the guys from school would see him driving it. He didn't like loaning out the Fairlane, but Mr. Pugh had insisted. And the money he was paying would buy Eddie that new carburetor. Surprisingly Dad had let him off, even though it meant Dad's having to interrupt working on the Lincoln to wait on gas customers.

"Go ahead, Eddie," he had said. "Mr. Pugh's a good customer. We better keep him happy."

The banker had some funny notions, insisting his yard be mowed this very afternoon and paying Eddie way more than the going rate, especially since the lawn didn't even look ragged yet. The guy's wife had just died—why was he so worried about his grass?

"Folks don't all grieve the same, son," Dad had said when Eddie asked him that.

So Eddie had obediently gone to the Pugh home, taken the lawnmower out, added oil and adjusted the spark. But after going over half the yard—could you call it mowing when you didn't cut much of anything?—the machine ran out of fuel. A gas can in the garage proved to be empty. Eddie considered not doing the rest, since it wouldn't look much different anyway, but decided not to chance it.

He then went back to the station, calling out to Dad in the mechanic's bay that it was him, refilled the can and started back to finish the well-paying job. Ahead of him, he saw Miss Wills's Chevy and wondered why she would be out of the library this time of day.

Eddie wanted to talk to her, to ask if she believed Rev. Asher had been as bad as the message on the church wall said. If so, what did she think ought to have been done about him?

That question might tip her Eddie knew something about the minister's death, but she already thought that. The question bothered him a lot lately. If someone was a tool of Satan, and you knew it, surely you should do something about it. But was beating the man up in a church—the same one he pastored—the right thing to do?

He wanted to tell her the truth about the alibi. If only it wasn't Gib who was involved.

Miss Wills's car reached Fourth Street, where Eddie should turn to go to Pugh's house. She continued on, and impulsively he did also. Maybe Miss Wills would pull into the Dairy Queen at the edge of town, he thought. He would happen to stop there too, they would get to talking about weather and school and then he would ask what she thought about Rev. Asher.

But she didn't slow at the Dairy Queen, in fact speeded up. He knew he ought to get back to the mowing job, necessary or not, but decided to go a little farther. He seldom got loose on his own this time of day, and it felt good to be out driving around.

They approached the G.O.L. farm. Eddie decided he would go just past it, then turn. But wait. Miss Wills was slowing—maybe she was turning back herself. What should he do, reverse directions first, or continue on and pass her?

But the Chevy veered to the right, bumped through the farm entrance and up the gravel road. Eddie noticed the gate was gaping wide, which usually happened only at G.O.L. meeting times. Startled, he let the pickup wander into the other lane, barely missing a new Lexus that swept past, its driver glaring.

Eddie drove beyond the gate, pivoted and crept slowly back, trying to think what this development meant. Surely Miss Wills couldn't know this was G.O.L. headquarters. But why else would she come? *No one* should be here now.

Impetuously Eddie drove in too.

Staying well behind Miss Wills, he entered the dense woods. Car lights flicked on ahead, but he didn't risk using his.

At last he came out into the compound and paused at its edge. In the parking lot near the office, Miss Wills's car sat, lights now off. He didn't see her anywhere.

Hold on. Beside her Chevy sat his own blue Fairlane. Stranger yet. Was Mr. Pugh out here too? He had no connection with G.O.L. either. The banker seemed full of surprises: hiring Eddie to mow a lawn that didn't need it, insisting on borrowing the Ford, now turning up here at headquarters.

Unsure what he would find ahead, Eddie decided against proceeding on to the parking lot. Instead, he stopped beside the arena where he and other trainees sometimes fought with pugil sticks. He got out and sauntered to the office, feeling protective of the place. Three people out here, and only he belonged. He wasn't exactly supposed to be here himself on a Friday afternoon, but had more right than the others.

But who had opened the gate? And why were these two here? Had G.O.L.'s cover been penetrated? Nervously, Eddie approached the office building.

Chapter Thirty-five

"Eddie—" Juanita murmured, glancing about as though expecting to spot the teenager in a wastebasket or a drawer. The small room was bare of furniture save for the desk and three chairs.

And bare of Eddie.

She looked back at Pugh, who still wore a broad smile. The hand holding the pistol gripped it lightly but confidently. Her racing heart dropped to her toes.

"Afternoon, Miss Wills. So glad you could join me."

"Eddie," Juanita inanely repeated.

"As you have guessed by now, Miss Wills, young Mr. Wagoner won't be joining us. Using his backwards 'E' in that note to you was a particularly nice touch, wasn't it?"

If only she had listened to her subconscious, Juanita thought. It had suspected the note was a trap, had made her call Wayne, look for Eddie in town, had even tried to keep her from entering this house.

"That was your white car Bud was working on," she said tonelessly. "You borrowed Eddie's and got him out of the way in case I should go by the station to look for him."

"Very good, Miss Wills."

"But your note said I had followed him out here. How in the world did you know that?"

"Walt Fuller told me. He was driving to last Monday's meeting when he saw both you and Eddie ahead. After Eddie turned in here, you drove back and forth past the place, so Walt figured you were suspicious. You were so intent on the gate you didn't even notice Walt pulling off the road a ways back to watch you." Pugh motioned to two chairs side by side on a wall.

Juanita sat in one. Walt Fuller—so she had been right about

him. She started to ask a question, but stopped as a floorboard creaked in the hallway. Pugh trained the gun on the door, still managing to watch Juanita. They waited.

The door opened. Eddie stepped in. At sight of the weapon, his eyes flew wide. He looked at Juanita as if for explanation. She could only stare at him, speechless.

"Come in, Eddie," Pugh said. "Why are you here? Did you by chance follow Miss Wills?"

Eddie looked from the banker to Juanita and back again, his expression both puzzled and frightened. Slowly, he nodded.

"Take a seat by her, young man. We're having a chat."

The teenager obeyed. Juanita had mixed emotions about his arrival. She hated seeing him in danger, but realized if she could make him understand what was going on, his wiry strength and young reflexes might prove useful.

"I assume you plan to kill me, Willard," she said. "Like you murdered your wife?"

"'By jove, I think she's got it!'" said Pugh in a horrendous imitation of Rex Harrison as Henry Higgins in "My Fair Lady." He sobered. "Actually, I regret this, Miss Wills. I had planned to let you live."

"You still can, Willard. We can work something out."

He didn't dignify the remark with a response.

"When did you come up with your plan to get rid of Estelle and have me convince the authorities I was the real target?"

Pugh smiled. "It came to me at Books the night after Asher's beating, when people were ribbing you about thinking yourself a detective. You were the key. I knew if I fed you enough intriguing clues I could count on you to snoop."

"Then your anonymous phone calls convinced me I had stumbled onto something that worried G.O.L. Getting Estelle to change shifts in the van with me must've involved luck, though."

He nodded. "Fortunately I was the one who got that call from the TV station, not her."

Keep him talking, Juanita thought, and think of a plan. "What's your connection to Guardians of Liberty, Willard?"

"Walt and I started it. I'd been worried about the path soft-headed liberals like Asher were taking the country down for a long time. But I had my position in the community to protect, so I've stayed in the background. Even militia members other than Walt don't know of my backing."

"How much did Asher know about G.O.L.?"

"I'm not sure—maybe more suspicions than certainty—but Walt heard about a sermon he preached against hate groups. Sounded like he knew something. Walt sent Jeffcoat to monitor him and called him anonymously a few times, trying to scare him into silence. Asher refused, and Walt got afraid he had recognized his voice and would tell authorities."

All at once Pugh's calm demeanor changed. His left hand scrubbed briskly at his thigh, and he seemed to quiver with excitement. He tittered shrilly, reminding Juanita of his unexpected giggle during her bank interview. She wondered if he was entirely sane.

"You fell beautifully for my plan," he went on, speaking rapidly now, "except for one thing. This morning you said some detail was nagging at you about the Asher matter, and I realized what you meant. I knew then I'd have to kill you."

Juanita's eyes swept the room, looking for a potential weapon, but saw only a pile of rope on the floor beside Pugh, as if he was planning to tie them up. She considered grabbing her purse off the floor by her chair and tossing it at the gun. But if Pugh noticed her reaching for it, he would probably shoot her immediately. Anyway, she had never been great at softball. Her throw might miss.

"What I was trying to recall," she said, "was something you

said at Books the Thoreau evening, that I was brave to go into the *dark* sanctuary. The paper didn't mention the lights were off when I went in, and they'd been turned on by the time the ambulance attendants arrived. You had to have heard that detail from one of the vandals themselves."

Pugh's mouth twitched. "Walt had given me a full report of the evening, including how pissed-off he was at Cooper. I realized immediately I had made a slip, but figured you hadn't noticed." His thigh-rubbing slowed. He alternately grinned and frowned.

"It was a brilliant plan, Willard. Don't spoil everything now by more killing."

"This'll work out. When your bullet-riddled bodies are found, people will think G.O.L. succeeded in its second attempt to kill you and that Eddie unfortunately happened to be with you." He sounded resigned, a reluctant murderer forced to slay more foolish victims.

Juanita looked at Eddie, whose lean face held a mixture of emotions. She guessed he was trying not to cry. Maybe she could pretend to hear a noise outside, then pounce on Pugh when he turned to look. Eddie and she together could overpower such a small man. But would the boy help? Could he?

"You realize they'll trace that pistol to you."

Pugh snorted, then gave a high-pitched, unnatural snicker. "They won't, actually. It's Cooper's. Earl Trevethan told me about his Vietnam stuff, so I dropped by and asked to see it. Cooper was flattered, didn't even notice me palming this." The banker transferred the gun to his left hand, flexed the right and changed back.

"Cooper will get blamed for four deaths—Asher's, Estelle's, yours and young Mr. Wagoner's." Pugh thoughtfully tapped a fingertip against his teeth. "There's even an excellent reason for Eddie to die. He was about to confess helping Cooper fake his alibi, you see, and Cooper shot him to prevent that. Yes, it all dovetails nicely."

Juanita looked at Eddie again, saw him fidget in his chair, heightened color creeping upward from his neck. He appeared angry. Come to think of it, the news they were about to be killed ticked her off too.

Now she had a new worry. Suppose Eddie in youthful exuberance hurled himself at the banker, but miscalculated. He might hasten both their deaths.

She craved every precious second she had left.

Chapter Thirty-six

Eddie's mouth felt parched as old bones. At first he had thought the pistol a joke, but Mr. Pugh's actions and talk said otherwise. He had been so nice earlier about that job, now he came across as a terrible guy. It all seemed to have something to do with his wife getting blown up last night.

Time shifted to slow motion. The banker's words floated past Eddie like bubbles from a kid's pipe. Action movies, TV programs, even G.O.L. mock battles—nothing had prepared Eddie to calmly face a real gun barrel at close range. His eyes fastened on a corner of the desk, scored deeply many times with a pocket knife. Someone had once sat there bored beyond measure and taking it out on the furniture. Eddie knew his brain should be in overdrive, figuring how to disarm the enemy and protect Miss Wills. But his mind refused to register anything except his own terror and the corner of a stupid desk.

He also felt an uncomfortable sensation in his groin, an urge to use the bathroom. Another sign this was real life. Screen heroes never peed their pants.

"Cooper—" The name leaped from Mr. Pugh's drifting words. The gun he held belonged to Gib, he was saying, and Gib would get blamed for all the murders.

That wasn't fair. Gib had been wrong to beat up the preacher, Eddie had decided, but shouldn't get framed for stuff he didn't do.

Mr. Pugh got up, took a length of cord from a heap on the floor and tossed it to Miss Wills.

"I thought these old pieces of rope might come in handy. Tie Eddie in his chair if you please, Miss Wills. Arms behind him, nice and tight. Don't get any ideas about leaving him wiggle room."

If Eddie were going to do anything, it would have to happen before she finished tying him. He watched Miss Wills closely, hoping she would signal what he should do. Sweat drenched her forehead. Her eyes bored into his. Eddie couldn't tell if her intent look directed him to tackle Mr. Pugh or stay put.

It didn't matter, he realized. He felt welded to his chair, unable to move.

Following the banker's instructions, Miss Wills wrapped the rope several times around Eddie's arms and knotted it firmly. Then she sat again, no longer looking at him. Whatever she had tried to tell him with that piercing gaze no longer mattered.

He felt relieved to be tied, no longer under an obligation to act. But that left everything up to Miss Wills. Unless she could somehow outsmart Mr. Pugh, there would soon be two dead bodies here. And one would be wearing wet pants.

Chapter Thirty-seven

Pugh checked Eddie's bonds and nodded his satisfaction. He stood above Juanita, his eyes glinting triumph as they looked down on her. He held the pistol so tightly the knuckles of his hand gleamed white. No longer the sedate, controlled banker, he looked nervy to the point of hysteria.

Juanita felt keyed up herself, her anxiety at its zenith. Somehow she must prevent Pugh's tying her too.

"There are some things I don't understand, Willard," she said quickly. "You planted clues implicating various people in Wyndham. Why didn't you just make everything point to Cooper, since you're making him your fall guy anyway?"

He giggled.

That odd reaction again, Juanita thought. Mere nervousness, or was Pugh on the verge of breakdown?

"I couldn't risk making the trail too obvious," he said with a snicker. "You might've seen through it. Plus I figured it'd be more fun for you if you got to suspect lots of people." He sat again, relaxing slightly against the wall.

"Thanks. So kind of you. Incidentally, the lychee nuts were too much. Way over the top."

Pugh chortled. "Every clue couldn't be a gem. But you believed a lot of them, didn't you?"

Juanita glanced at Eddie. A stony mask hid whatever emotions he felt. But he did seem to have understood her look warning him against rash action. Returning her gaze to Pugh, she noticed a triangular hole in the window behind his head. It must be true that danger heightened one's awareness of small details. At least the banker seemed calmer. But enough for her to catch him off guard? Keep him talking, she reminded herself.

"The bookmark in Boston's book was an especially clever

clue. Roy isn't actually in G.O.L., is he?"

"Certainly not. But I loved making you think he was. And after learning you liked ciphers, I couldn't resist giving you one to solve."

"That easy code didn't show much confidence in my skills as a cryptographer. I don't suppose G.O.L. really passes messages that way?"

Pugh laughed scornfully. "Hardly. But when I was planning clues to give you, I recalled a harebrained idea Walt had when he and I first talked about founding Guardians of Liberty. He wanted us to use 'secret codes' to communicate with each other. I'm afraid Walt's a little boy in some ways. He talks tough, but really just likes strutting around being the 'Major.' That's one of the reasons G.O.L. doesn't work. That and antics by hotdogs like Cooper, which would've brought the authorities in sooner or later."

"So you figured even G.O.L. was expendable in a good cause, like murdering your wife."

"Since it couldn't have lasted anyway, why not use it?"

"You're something, Willard. I don't know enough obscenities to say what. I suppose you planted that 'orgies' rumor too?"

Pugh grinned, working his fist energetically against his thigh. Juanita wondered if the hand was going to sleep or if he was releasing tension.

"Yes, and that was easy. I told it to a woman who uses the same beauty shop as Estelle. So you actually heard the rumor from Estelle, and I 'confirmed' it later. I knew you wouldn't buy the 'orgies' bit, but figured if you heard of something odd happening at Darrow's place you'd connect him with G.O.L. Can't stand that guy—his politics make Ralph Nader's seem reasonable. I enjoyed sending you after him."

Juanita shifted uneasily in her chair. It was a fascinating discussion, but knowing she would die at its end definitely lessened her enjoyment.

Pugh abruptly sat up, fished with his free hand among the jumble of cord and extracted another strand. He rose and strode toward Juanita, pistol in one hand, rope in the other.

"Hands behind your back. Together."

Juanita obeyed. As he leaned to wrap the line around her wrists, fumbling one-handedly, she caught a whiff of wintergreen, a light clean odor at odds with his evil actions. She considered trying to wrest the weapon from him. But with both man and pistol behind her, she might screw up, and the struggle could send a bullet into either her or Eddie.

The gun bumped coldly against her arm as the banker's right hand assisted his left, looping the rope twice around her wrists and pulling it snug. Then holding it taut with his left hand, he bent to lay the gun on the floor.

Her last chance. Juanita pushed hard with her legs, forcing her chair backward into him. She jerked her wrists, yanking the rope from his hands.

He sprang away from the thrust and shoved the chair forward. It dropped hard, jarring Juanita. His fist slammed truncheon-like into her skull. Her head drooped forward, throbbing from the impact. While she sat half-stunned, Pugh grabbed her hands and tightened the rope around them.

"Why'd you—think you had to—kill Estelle, Willard?" she managed to ask, desperately hoping even now to distract him and gain an advantage. "Divorce is—pretty simple these days."

"My dear Miss Wills," he said patronizingly, his fingers busy tying a knot, "Estelle and her father would never have stood for a divorce. She didn't care a fig about me, but loved the status of being a banker's wife. If I'd filed for divorce, Daddy would have destroyed me."

In her semi-dazed state, Juanita could tell Pugh's hasty trussing was leaving some play in her bonds. Given sufficient time, she could probably work her hands loose. But she doubted she would get that. A glance at Eddie showed naked fear in his eyes.

"It was a matter of money too," Pugh said, returning to the heaped cable. "The investments Estelle and her daddy made didn't include me. In a divorce I'd have been cut out."

"But you do benefit from her death?"

Pugh chose a length of rope, discarded it and picked another. "Estelle was old-fashioned enough to leave everything to her husband. Her entire share comes to me."

He tied Juanita's feet to the chair legs. Then picking another cord from among the snarls, he knelt beside Eddie and began wrapping it around his legs. The boy didn't look at him, or at Juanita. The banker had become less agitated, but she wasn't sure which was more dangerous—a shaky, nervous Pugh or a coldly calculating one. She heard their captor's quick breathing, the rubbing of rope on rope.

Faint sounds of something moving through brush came from outside. A wild animal? Or a human?

Springing into action, Pugh dropped the rope, whipped a handkerchief from his windbreaker pocket and fastened it about Juanita's lips, so snugly she couldn't move them. He rummaged through his pants pockets, checked Eddie's garments and found a hanky in a pocket of the boy's jeans jacket. He tied it over the lad's mouth.

Juanita heard the low noises again, skirting the house on the parking-lot side near the room they were in. Pugh crept to the wall beside the window and peered out, careful not to show himself. His mouth widened in a leer that again made Juanita question his sanity.

Creeping back to her chair, he whispered, "Your boyfriend. He's out there, hiding behind a big rock. I'll give him a surprise."

Wayne! Relief and joy filled Juanita. Then fear returned,

heightened by worry for him. Pugh might kill all three of them.

Clutching his pistol, Pugh stole from the room and softly shut the door. Juanita heard the hall floor squeak as he moved toward the front entrance.

She pondered her fix. The tight gag wouldn't let her call a warning to Wayne. Still, that could be a good thing. If he heard her voice but didn't understand the words, he would be watching this room instead of looking about outside, where the peril would be.

Juanita visualized the house from the front. Dense underbrush hugged it on the right, so Pugh would have to circle the vehicles on the parking lot to reach Wayne. If only she could direct her darling's eyes to the area of danger.

She tested her ropes. A bit slack. She could probably wriggle loose, in time. But Wayne didn't have time.

An idea occurred. She groped backward and downward toward her purse. Her fingers pawed air. She tried again, straining all her muscles, but still couldn't reach the bag.

Panic gripped her. In her mind, she saw Pugh steal toward Wayne, his small body hidden by her Chevy's metal shell. Unless Wayne happened to look that way and saw him—

No! There had to be a way. She glanced at Eddie, whose frightened eyes stared at her from above the tight kerchief. Then she realized the cord encircling his legs was still untied. She head-gestured toward her pocketbook, jiggling up and down in her frustration.

Finally, understanding dawned in his eyes. He scooted his chair around till his cowboy boots touched the leather. Shifting the purse with one foot, he hooked its strap with the sharp toe of the other. Carefully he lifted the bag and held it near her hands.

Juanita grabbed the pocketbook and inched it around till one bound hand felt its fastener. She pushed. Abruptly, the purse opened. She froze, terrified of dropping it.

Slowly, carefully, she maneuvered a hand inside. Her exploring fingers found the remote, drew it forth and dropped the bag. Holding the control as near the window as her tied hands allowed, she pressed its switch. If only the Chevy would start now, of all times.

The car engine roared, the siren shrilled. Beautiful sounds.

A gun fired. Then two more shots, a different sound. The first weapon again. Then silence.

Eddie and Juanita stared at each other wide-eyed, her heart doing loops.

At last the front door opened. Someone came along the hallway, making no effort to avoid the telltale boards.

Wayne? Or Pugh?

Chapter Thirty-eight

Juanita eyed the door, dreading for it to open. But as the steps came closer, she realized they sounded too heavy for Pugh. Her heart's frantic thumping slowed.

The door swung back. Wayne walked in carrying a rifle, a walking jungle in camouflage shirt and pants. His solemn expression changed as he saw Juanita in her bound state, obviously unharmed except for her dignity.

"Juanita, you're looking especially lovely," he said with a grin. "How's tricks, Eddie? Tell me about your day, babe. Don't leave out any details."

Above the gag, her eyes narrowed menacingly. Wayne laid down his rifle, knelt and reached for the handkerchief's ends. Then he paused, drew back.

"I don't know. Pretty peaceful in here. Maybe I'll untie Eddie first, make a few calls, write out a report."

Her gaze turned murderous. Chuckling, he finished his task. The gag had left the lower part of her face numb, and Juanita worked her lips around before trying to talk.

"It's you," she said unnecessarily. "Where's Pugh?"

"I've gotten warmer receptions from damsels I've rescued."

He hugged her, ropes and all, and kissed her so hard all feeling left her lips again. He smelled of perspiration and dust, her favorite odors at the moment.

"Pugh's dead," he said simply.

Wayne removed Eddie's gag. "Thanks," the boy said, his first word since entering the room.

Wayne untied the ropes from their hands, and both rubbed their wrists.

"I've never been so glad to see anybody, Wayne," Juanita admitted, "but how did you—"

Wayne kissed her forehead. "You were so sure something

was fishy here, I decided to check it out. I couldn't officially investigate, but figured if I went hunting on my own time and wandered onto the land by mistake—. The fellow who owns the adjacent property gave me permission to hunt there, and I slipped onto this farm from the rear."

He began on the ropes around her legs. She snuggled against his shoulder.

"I am so glad to see you, Wayne."

"Keep that in mind for tonight. Good thing you started that car when you did. I turned to look just as Pugh came around the fender. Sure wasn't expecting to see him out here. 'Course with that gun trained on me, I didn't wait for a formal explanation."

"He set me up, Wayne. I hate getting conned, and he did an exceptionally good job of it."

Wayne's eyebrows drew together. "You'll have to explain that later, babe. Eddie, you have some talking to do too, son." He stood and glanced around. "I saw a phone line coming into this room." Searching desk drawers, he located an old-style black instrument.

While he was phoning, Juanita rose and stretched. She turned to Eddie, who looked relieved but wary, pulled him to his feet and embraced him.

"It's okay now, Eddie. We're safe. Whatever you've been mixed up in, it's over."

The boy eyed her from a six-inch height advantage, emotions chasing across his slender face. Juanita realized he might not see the demise of G.O.L. as good news.

As she watched him, a slow grin started. Thin arms stole around Juanita's waist, and Eddie Wagoner hugged her too.

Chapter Thirty-nine

Saturday evening Juanita threw an impromptu dinner party at her home, inviting Wayne, Eva and Cyril, Katherine, Doug, Meador, Mavis, the Nguyens and Eddie Wagoner. As they sat in the living room before the meal, Eddie dribbled iced tea on a couch, blushed crimson and stammered an apology. Juanita fetched a towel and wiped up the liquid.

"Don't worry about it, Eddie. This fabric's like iron—nothing stains it."

He hadn't wanted to come, but she had talked him into it. Now she could practically hear him counting off seconds before he could leave.

"See, people didn't even notice," she said, gesturing down the long room.

That was nearly true. Wayne was telling the Bromptons about new video cameras the police department was getting. Doug, Meador and Tinh discussed a basketball game they had seen on TV. Katherine urged Bach to take an English as a Second Language class at the community college. Eva stood at the bay window watching the Nguyen children play with Rip in the yard.

Only Mavis had noticed the gaffe. She came to sit beside Eddie, while Juanita prepared to defend him against her tongue-lashing. But her colleague surprised her.

"Willie, my youngest, is always spilling things too," Mavis said, "but doesn't mean to. He's the sweetest boy. So good-natured."

As Eddie shyly ducked his head, Juanita wondered where Willie had found a role model for his temperament. Maybe in the reclusive *Mr.* Ralston?

"Willie's my favorite," Mavis went on. "He lives in Claremore now, but comes to see me often."

Leaving Eddie to deal with the unexpectedly gentle attention, Juanita set spaghetti, sauces, salad and garlic bread on a buffet in the breakfast nook adjacent to the kitchen. The diners filled plates and sat either at a round oak table in the nook or on stools at kitchen counters and stove. Mavis ladled food generously onto Eddie's plate and found them places at a counter. The teenager followed docilely.

"This clam sauce is wonderful, Juanita," Eva said as they sat with Cyril and Katherine at the table. "You know, I can't get over the fact Willard killed Estelle. I always thought he was a nasty little man, but not a murderer."

"Never can tell about people, Eva," Doug said from a place beside the range. "Who knows what your dear husband is capable of, for instance?"

Eva eyed her husband fondly. "Cyril has no secrets from me. Though he may think he has."

Cyril glanced up, and Juanita saw a look pass between the couple. Cyril turned pink and shoved a forkful of pasta into his mouth, red sauce dribbling down his chin.

"You're one to talk, Doug," Juanita said. "Isn't it time you and Meador tell what you get up to Monday evenings?"

Doug glanced at Meador. The younger man's eyes widened, but he shrugged his shoulders. Nodding, Doug laid down his napkin. "Okay, the fellows wanted to keep it quiet, but with all the rumors going around—. Actually, I've been teaching a self-defense class out at my place."

"Self-defense?" Juanita stared at Meador. "Is that what all those fighting quotes were about?"

He grinned sheepishly. "After I learned a few tactics, I started to get really interested. Guess I got a little carried away."

"A little?" Mavis hooted. "General Patton lives."

"And you're believable as a peacemaker, aren't you?"

"Neither of you advanced the cause of pacifism," Juanita observed. "Help yourself to more food, everyone."

"It's real good, Miss Wills," Eddie said, grinning as Mavis heaped more spaghetti on his plate.

"How did you figure out it was Mr. Pugh, Miss Wills?" Katherine asked.

"I didn't for a long time." Juanita explained Pugh's "dark sanctuary" slip and her realization that Estelle could have been the intended victim all along. "Willard didn't care who I thought was guilty, so long as he wasn't the one."

She added hot bread to the basket, and Eva and Cyril freshened drinks. Juanita took advantage of their absence to whisper to Katherine, "I even wondered about you for a time."

Katherine's eyes grew round behind their strong lenses. "You suspected me of Mrs. Pugh's murder? Why?"

"Not of that, but I decided you must have inside knowledge of a local militia. You seemed more sure than most that there'd be such a group here."

"Oh, that." Katherine smiled sadly. "When I was a child, my father and racist friends of his used to say things like, 'Niggers and Jews need taking down a peg.' Nobody mentioned the Klan, but that must be the way such organizations get started."

Eva returned to her seat. "All I can say, Juanita, is, you were mighty fortunate Wayne showed up."

"And I'm lucky she started the Chevy when she did," Wayne said from a chair at a counter.

"Eddie's the real hero," Juanita said. "If he hadn't figured out I needed my purse and passed it to me, none of us would be here."

The teen flushed and hung his head, but a smile tugged at his lips. Mavis gave him a congratulatory backslap. "How's about we do dishes, Mr. Hero?"

He nodded. While the others cleared, Juanita prepared dishwater and handed Eddie a towel. She poured coffee, and all except the cleanup crew retired to the living room. She couldn't hear the low conversation in the kitchen, but Eddie's easy stance suggested he was more comfortable with Mavis than with Edith Wagoner.

Mavis had certainly revealed a new side of herself. Perhaps she didn't really deserve to be drowned in pig's urine as had seemed the case yesterday, Juanita reflected.

"Juanita told me about that letter and the garbage thrown at your house," Wayne said to Tinh. "If you have any more trouble, be sure and tell the police. It's what we're here for."

Bach touched Tinh's arm and spoke in Vietnamese, words Juanita suspected would roughly translate as "I told you so."

Tinh looked at Juanita and back at Wayne. "In my country, police not need help from librarians." A hint of a smile played about his lips.

The fiber from the bush at the church matched a sweater belonging to Jeffcoat. He and Fuller tried to outdo each other telling all. Arrests of Guardians of Liberty members—Cooper, Fuller, Jeffcoat and others involved in various weapons thefts—put the organization out of business. For the present. Under that particular name.

Someone on Jesse Shipman's team (Roy Boston, Juanita guessed) obtained proof that Virg Piersall and Earl Trevethan had put out the scurrilous anti-Piersall poster. Once that dirty trick had been exposed, voters turned to Shipman in droves. Whether his victory would be good for the county, time would tell.

Eddie got a "B+" on his English paper. He came to the library to show it to Juanita, eyes dancing with happiness. "Mr. Darrow's helped me lots in history too," he said. "I think maybe I'm gonna graduate."

"What will you do then, Eddie?"

"Dunno, maybe join the army." He hesitated. "Or I might be a cop like Mr. Cleary."

"Whatever you do, I hope you'll be successful and happy. You're a terrific young man. And don't let anyone tell you different."

The flu bug that had swept through the Wyndham Police Department ran its course. Juanita and Wayne saw each other more often and found the time together sweeter for having nearly lost each other. She still didn't like his dangerous occupation, but as he triumphantly pointed out she had risked her own life when investigating wasn't even her job. However, she actually got him to admit her nosiness sometimes had good results.

"Of course," he added, "if you ever do anything like this again, I'll personally flay the hide right off you."

Since he was nuzzling the back of her neck at the time, she didn't take the threat too seriously.

— THE END —

1062669

Made in the USA